BRIDES OF RIVERSIDE

A HISTORICAL MAIL ORDER BRIDE SERIES

FAITH-ANN SMITH

Copyright © 2015-2019 by Faith-Ann Smith
www.hopemeadowpublishing.com

All rights reserved. Printed in the United States of America. No part of this book may be used or reproduced in any manner whatsoever without written permission except in the case of brief quotations embodied in critical articles or reviews.

This book is a work of fiction. Names, characters, businesses, organizations, places, events and incidents either are the product of the author's imagination or are used fictitiously. Any resemblance to actual persons, living or dead, events, or locales is entirely coincidental.

CONTENTS

MAIL ORDER BRIDE: WILLOW

BRIDES OF RIVERSIDE

CHAPTER 1

BATH, MAINE. JUNE, 1895.

LILY BARRINGTON HELD HER BREATH, HER STOMACH tied in impossible knots; not the good, warm, fuzzy, hopeful kind, but the kind you felt when your world tumbled on its head. She leaned forward, teetering to the edge of a creaking chair, her eyes glued to her sister's face.

Over a gigantic lump lodged in her throat, her words trickled out and rent the air. "Willow, the bank cannot take this house. It's the only place we have. Cousin Raymond left it for us when he went to India, and he promised we could stay here forever. If the bank takes our home, where will we go?"

The strident cry filled the atmosphere with

repressed tension, and a dark cloud hovered over the gray-papered walls and dust filled chandelier. The open window, set to the east, allowed a cool summer air to circulate, but the acrid taste of the day's events left little to be desired.

Willow, the eldest of three girls, tried to inject a voice of optimism to offset the sense of helplessness. With a determined glint in her gray-blue eyes, she dismissed Lily's frantic concerns with a stiff upper lip. "We'll do what the Barrington family does well: rise from the ashes and blossom in the light. It's what Mother and Father taught us: to keep our chin above the tide."

Rose—the youngest of the Barrington clan— smiled with a sad face and muttered, "That's why we lost our family fortune. Because our parents wanted to build ships in the dead of winter and sail them around the world. Both ships were smashed, and now we are destitute and adrift. I daresay we're a ship without an anchor or a captain."

Willow grimaced at the frank statement and conceded her sister's point. But she didn't want them to wallow in despair, or lose their sense of confidence. "Mistakes do not have to control our future. We can do much better. I know we can."

Wonder reflected in her turquoise gaze, and Rose

championed Willow's staunch fortitude: "That's the spirit, and I admire it. But when we're starving, what will we do? If we end up in the poor house I know you'll change your tune."

Willow gnawed the edge of her lips, her cheeks pale in a sharp face framed by sun kissed waves. She wished she had the answers to her sister's questions, but she didn't. Her mother always told her, "If wishes were horses, beggars would ride," and the statement held true. Willow accepted that if she could wish her life to be different, things might be different after all.

Her gaze wandered to her sisters Lily and Rose. She'd do her best to see them safe, but she needed a much higher power to carry that out.

Willow had spent most of her life caring for her siblings. Her parents had been so busy racing after either one scheme or another that they had no time for three young children. So, Willow stepped in and became a substitute mother—and father.

The result was a steadfast young woman with solemn eyes, who wore a mantle of seriousness that clung to her gaunt frame. A nonexistent bust line made her appear younger than her thirty-two years, but she thought little of her female attributes—or lack of it. Concern for her sisters' welfare had consumed her life and left room for little else.

Her thoughts turned to a passage of the Bible she had read earlier. She knew great wisdom could be gleaned from its pages. "Let's imitate Gideon, the mighty one who defeated an army with only three hundred men."

Rose smiled with a pained expression. She tossed her waist-length blonde plait over her shoulder and said, "Willow, Gideon did not defeat the army alone. He had divine intervention to help him, remember?" She strolled toward the center of the room and crouched next to the low-lying table. "Let us gather at this round table and channel King Arthur's knights. It might inspire us to come up with an idea."

Willow appreciated her younger sister's humorous stance, but Lily brimmed with continued fear. "We are pitted against a fate worse than death. Why can't you see that?"

Willow groaned and turned to her with a wry glance. "Stop piling on the waterworks, dearest. I swear you have streams of water for eyes."

When Lily's wails strummed to the tune of a howling operetta, Rose interjected a voice of reason to calm the tension in the air. "Lily, calm yourself, please." Then she turned to Willow with a curious glance, "You must have a modicum of feelings on the matter. How can you be so calm? It is indecent."

Willow ran her hands over the folds of her dress. The faded print and lavender patches resembled a garment more suitable for a scullery maid, but she had no eye for fine clothing, nor could she afford it. "I am very affected, dear Rose, but I refuse to let life cast me into a mire of despondent dreams. Tears will not feed us in the days to come."

Her gentle reprimand had the desired effect. Lily lowered her head and dried her red-rimmed eyes. Unable to see a positive road ahead, she sought to explain the reason for her fears. "We have no skills other than housekeeping. How will we live?"

Good question. Willow sighed and took a deep breath, prepared to spread more misfortune. "There are more pressing matters to consider."

When her sisters turned to her with grave faces, Willow shared the contents of the letter she had received that morning. "I got a letter from our aunt today. She said Mama and Papa can stay with her in London under the care of a nurse. The pneumonia has gotten worse. The doctor said they must have excellent care. So, we need to send whatever coin we can, and as often as we can."

Lily tumbled to the floor, her eyes wide and troubled. This new detail could not be ignored. "Willow, please let me go to the fishery to work. My hands are strong and I don't mind hard labor. They pay well and we need the money."

Willow rejected the idea with a firm headshake before it took hold. She had heard of fever and cholera outbreaks often, and couldn't bear the thought of more illness in the family. "No, Lily. We must keep our jobs at the bakery. It will tide us over until we find something better."

Rose didn't agree with Willow's persistent viewpoint. "Not enough to keep our heads above water. We must act now, or I'm afraid it *will* be the poor house—or worse."

CHAPTER 2

WILLOW STROLLED ACROSS THE WOODEN FLOOR, THE folds of her skirt rustling along the split beams. She lit the side lamps with deft hands and glanced at the fireplace. The faint embers stirred, but she didn't have the heart to stoke it further.

It had been a tiresome day, and the meeting at the bank left her exhausted and shattered. One step into the cloistered office, which resembled a square box with bare furnishings and stark walls, had brought her face to face with a flint-nosed agent. He glared over his spectacles and regarded her as a soiled shade teetered to an unwashed lamp. When she sat without his permission, he shot her a flat, friendless smile.

Subdued by his brusque demeanor, Willow tried

to make the best of it, but her amiable nature crumbled when he explained their finances. In precise tones, he told her the bank planned to repossess the house unless she paid the back taxes.

The nebulous haze had since faded, but the sense of despair lingered in her mind. A well-to-do suitor might save them, but she dreaded the demands of a marriage union. To join her life to another and slave away for their contentment didn't suit her temperament. A determined spinster was more her cup of tea.

Should they return home in disgrace? The idea held for one moment and fragmented into impossible scenarios. When she digested the issue for the hundredth time, Willow lowered her head and tears trickled over her pale cheeks. *Dear Lord, please help us.*

CHAPTER 3

RIVERSIDE, CALIFORNIA

JOSHUA ADJUSTED HIS TAUT FRAME TO THE SLEEK wooden chair centered in the heart of the drawing room. He gazed at his father under lowered lids and wondered what new tricks the old geezer had churning in his mind.

Despite the unorthodox summons—at the edge of a gun barrel from a hired hand—Joshua was glad to see him. He felt proud to know his father could still command a crowd with his decisive presence and no-nonsense gaze.

Joshua admitted his father was not the only one blessed by good looks. Wallace males had tall, muscular frames and hewn shoulders, courtesy of hard work. They had compelling eyes—tender one moment and turbulent the next—with stalwart chins and personalities to match.

"When are you coming home, boy? This house is big enough for the family, last time I checked. We've got...must be... ten bedrooms in this place, unless your mother plans to add more."

Horton Wallace's gruff demand didn't dent Joshua's mood. No matter how much his father growled, Joshua knew he loved him. But he had a point.

His gaze wandered in nonchalant fashion to the gleaming light fixture with three lamps. The oval ceiling with crisscrossed wooden beams and intricate lacework appeared solid, but it didn't appeal to him. A davenport desk nestled in the corner looked nice, but he didn't have the temperament to sit and write letters. Curling flames in the cast iron fireplace enhanced its decorative mantelpiece, but it couldn't rival the molten glory of the evening sun. And the piano stood in the corner with bated breath, but he couldn't carry a tune to save his life.

In Joshua's view, nothing in his father's home compared to the open plains under a cerulean sky and cumulus clouds drifting in the summer breeze.

"Maybe I will come back if you don't send a gunslinger to fetch me."

Wallace grinned, with a twinkle in his eye. "You evaded my summons for three months, so I got to thinking. Glad to see it worked. So, when are you coming home?"

Joshua sighed at the unsubtle nature of his father's actions, but noted the obvious. "Why do you keep asking me that? I love the woods and my log cabin. If I moved back to Riverside, I'd die a slow death from rampant boredom."

Wallace dismissed his excuse with a grunt. "That log cabin is just an overgrown tree with windows and nothing else. Besides, it's too crowded. It must be six or seven ragamuffin boys living there by now. Bet you don't even remember their names."

Joshua shifted, unwilling to concede his father's point. "There are five of them, and I have them numbered so I can remember them. Number 1 is a wild card. Hates clean clothes and loves to climb trees. Tried to break his head last week. Number 2 is more of a—"

"Rubbish! Who calls a child by a number? They belong on the reservation, not camping in that shed behind what you call a home. And where is that hound of yours? You'd better keep him out of your mother's kitchen."

Joshua groaned at the implied reprimand and jumped to his feet with a thud. He didn't want to upset his mother. Running Deer had been nothing but supportive, and she was the one reason he attempted civilized behavior. "He is a wolf, not a hound, and I better find him. He might terrorize the cook in the kitchen. Don't think he can get enough of her prairie chicken stew."

Wallace shook his head and rolled his eyes. "*You* will terrorize the cook when she gets a good look at you, and not your pet. You resemble an Indian brave with sunburnt skin, long hair, and sheepskin clothing. Why don't you change, shave, and cut your hair for dinner this evening?"

Joshua froze mid-step and eyed his father with suspicion. The air swirled to a standstill and his eyes narrowed. "Did you invite a scatterbrained female to dinner?"

Wallace planted a mulish look on his face and clenched his fist. "It is my duty to see my sons wed. Your mother wants grandchildren, and by stars, she will get them. And since your two brothers aren't doing a thing, you'll set the example."

Joshua groaned and slapped his forehead. His

father loved to make his life impossible. Why the old man refused to accept his independence boggled his mind. "I plan to build up my homestead near the Santa Ana River. I have a small bluff up that way and it offers a nice view of the mountains and overlooks the water. The boys and I are just fine, and we don't need a woolgathering female telling us what to do."

Wallace slid his chair back and rose to his feet with a thunderous glare. He stared at his son for a long moment. Then his moustache twitched. "Your mother wants you to find a good, upstanding woman to marry, and I agree with her. And if I have to take you to the altar at gunpoint, so help me, you're getting married. Do you hear what I say, boy?"

Disgusted at the outcome of his visit, Joshua stalked away without words of farewell. He stomped to the kitchen and tried to wrap his brain around his father's new plan. The roar in his ears fueled the rush of blood racing through his veins, and his gut burned. He had to find his mother and get her to change his father's mind. He dreaded the old man's rampant quest for a new daughter-in-law and wondered what he might do. *Oh God, please save me.*

CHAPTER 4

BATH, MAINE. ONE MONTH LATER.

"I CAN'T BELIEVE MY EYES."

Willow embraced the well-dressed visitor with a bright smile, hungry for any morsel of good news. Her heart bubbled over on seeing her childhood friend. "Eliza Walkerton, as I live and breathe. It is you!"

The vision in pink ribbons and lace ruffles grinned, eyes brimming with laughter. "I'm here in Maine for two days. Short business trip for my husband."

She glanced at Willow's hand and inquired with a mischievous glint, "Is there no gentleman in your life, dare I ask?"

Willow ushered Eliza into the parlor and guided her to a chair. "No, dear heavens. Perish the thought. Give me a moment to get you a spot of tea. I can't wait to listen to your news."

Eliza agreed, her bright gaze taking in the frayed chairs, lopsided paintings, and dust filled windows. She touched her fingertips together and a mysterious smile hovered at the edges of her mouth. "I'll be glad to share."

They caught up on old news and Willow delighted in stories of Eliza's triumph in the West. "You married a rancher and have an orange farm? I didn't know the orange business was that good."

Eliza set her teacup aside and sighed in contentment. "Yes. California is thriving on gold, but of a different kind. Our orange groves are full of good fruit with no seeds, which makes everyone love them. But enough of my adventures. Tell me your news, and leave nothing out."

Willow groaned, not eager to share her side of life. "Well, the truth is—"

"Willow, come right away!"

The front door slammed, reverberating throughout the house. Willow dashed to her feet, but before she could take two steps, her sisters rushed into the salon in a clatter. They greeted Eliza, but before they could explain, Lily burst into tears. "They let us—go. The bakery," she sniffled, "they said —they don't—need us anymore."

Willow gasped at Lily's wailing cry and turned to Rose in shock. "What do you mean, they let you go? It's my turn to go in tomorrow."

Rose placed a trembling hand over Willow's arm and squeezed. "They don't want you to come. They have found family members at much lower wages."

Willow struggled to understand, but couldn't wrap her mind around the latest string of misfortunes. "The bank only gave us two months, and one is gone. I will ask for two more months, but I don't think they'll give us much more than that. When they take the house, we'll be on the street."

To everyone's surprise, Eliza stepped in with a quiet offer. "I have the answer to your problem sitting in my handbag."

CHAPTER 5

WILLOW TOSSED AND TURNED, SLEEP FAR FROM HER mind. The shapeless nightgown rasped her slender frame, leaving it flushed and unsettled. Her body refused to succumb to sleep, and each breath shook raw nerves. Unable to rest, she made her way to the kitchen for a cool drink of water.

Rose sat in the semi-shadows, gazing into a cup of tea with a pensive expression. She glanced up when Willow appeared and said, "Trouble sleeping? Me too. Shall I pour you a cup of tea?"

Willow mumbled her thanks and slipped into the frigid chair with her head buried in her hands. "What are we going to do? I have been thinking and thinking it over until my head hurts. I can't believe what's happening to us. Do you think God is mad at me for something?"

Rose busied herself with the kettle, the tea leaves, and the blue willow teacups. She boiled the water, steeped the leaves, and prepared the brew. "Nonsense, Willow. The good Lord does not try us with evil things. Now drink this for strength. I added a lavender drop to calm your nerves."

Willow raised her head, grateful for Rose's kindness. "Thank you, dear sister. You're right; I shouldn't have said that."

After a gentle sip invigorated her bones, she murmured, "Did you know you are the most level-headed one of us?"

Rose brushed aside the compliment with a smile. "Nonsense. That's your job, and now we need you to do it again. Can you cast your inner desires to the wind and save our family?"

Willow rejected the idea with her heart despite the clamor in her head. She longed to help her family, but marry a stranger in California? "I can't marry a man I have never met."

Rose smiled at the innocent comment and then grew serious. "It happens day in and day out. No reason for it to stop now."

Willow jumped to her feet and paced across the

hardwood floor. "Rose, what do I know of a marriage union? The suitors that tried to court me left in anger. They said I am coldhearted and not fit for womanhood. Others used choice words I can't repeat. How can I hope to be a—"

Rose struck a sad face at her sister's struggle to explain her feelings. "Willow, those suitors know nothing of you, or your heart. You are one of the most warmhearted people I know, and I wish it didn't have to happen this way. But we have no choice. Please tell me, will you accept Eliza's offer? If it didn't call for the eldest, I'd take your place."

Willow's smile blossomed through tears, touched at her sister's willingness to supplant her. She pressed her hands against her temples and her mind cleared.

"Alright... I suppose I will accept."

CHAPTER 6

RIVERSIDE, CALIFORNIA

THE STRANGER RESEMBLED A FALLEN ANGEL, WITH A shadowed beard clinging to his firm jaw. When he strolled into the drawing room, Willow jumped to her feet, gathering her scattered thoughts together. She stood on aching legs, glad the train trip lay behind her.

The journey from Maine to California had taken what seemed like an eternity. Horton Wallace had insisted she rest for two days, and she appreciated his kindness. It had taken great courage to prepare her heart for the task ahead, but she sensed imbued strength after her prayers. The reason for the drastic changed in her life offered further incentive. Her sisters' livelihood depended on her, and she couldn't fail them.

When the stranger came forward, he extended his hand. Willow craned her neck, wondering who he was. The blend of green and sable highlights that stared back caught her unawares. Where did he get such eyes?

"So, you're Miss Willow Barrington. Must be a big change for you coming out here."

Willow ignored his hand and glanced over his shoulder, expecting a fine upstanding gentleman dressed in proper attire to show himself. "I am waiting for Mr. Joshua Wallace. Have you seen him?"

He kept his hand extended and flashed an unrepentant grin. "Joshua's the name, and a frontier life's the game."

Willow stepped back, shaken at his unorthodox speech pattern and the strange expression in his eyes. The determination in his gaze and the taut curve of his cheek left her breathless. It must be tiredness from the journey. "Joshua Wallace? Your father told me you are the most respectable of the lot. He must have been joking."

Her inadvertently dismissive tone hit deep. His

eyes narrowed, and he rocked back on his heels, his glance unreadable. "Miss Barrington, I don't want you here anymore than you want to be, but we are facing forces beyond our control. Here, allow me to run to the kitchen and find you something sweet to eat."

Then his eyes roved her gaunt cheeks, and he left with a murmured, "Think you need it."

Willow folded her legs. Ashamed to have acted in such an overbearing manner, she closed her eyes and pressed her fingers to her temples. How could she be so rude?

Ten minutes later, the sound of running feet reached her ears. When a gigantic bolt of white fur streaked across the room, she screamed.

The beast sniffed the air, and Willow scrambled to get up, holding her parasol with clammy hands. The beast stared into her eyes with an unblinking gaze and she held her breath.

"Be still, Shadow, or Miss Barrington might just faint away."

The creature ambled to his side when Joshua returned with a glass of milk and a plate of cookies. He set them on the table next to the Queen Anne chair and removed the parasol from Willow's shaking hands, giving her the milk and cookies.

When he left, Willow released a deep breath and stared at her hands. Milk and cookies. Did he think she was a child to be coddled?

After dinner that evening, Joshua cornered Willow on the front porch. His gaze took in the elegant upsweep of her silken hair, and how the sapphire dress with gold ribbons enhanced her ivory skin. It resembled one of his mother's dresses, and she wore it well. "You've met my brothers tonight. Still think I'm the worst one of the lot?"

Willow tilted her chin, her voice firm and unafraid. "I never said you were the worst one, Mr. Wallace."

Joshua grunted, but pressed the point. "You said my father must be joking when he said I was the most respectable son. That's saying the same thing."

She gasped at his flat statement and flushed. "I was tired and shouldn't have said it. I apologize; you have treated me with nothing but kindness, and I thank you."

Joshua didn't want to cause further upset and offered a gentleman's way out of the pickle. "I'll tell my father to call off the union and we'll quit as friends. Lots of men here need good wives. You might find one of them to be more to your taste."

Before she could respond, Joshua strode away in

haste. He wished the best for Willow in her quest to find a good husband.

As Joshua slept, a solid object pressed against his nose, tickling his hairs with a frigid breath. When he swiped at the offending object and it jabbed against his flesh for a second time, his eyes flew open. He groaned at the sight of the revolving cylinder of a Colt .45 staring him in the face. *Not again.*

"Sorry to wake you, Mr. Wallace." The cowhand grinned with gleaming eyes. "Your Pa says you're getting married today, and there's not much time left by the looks of things."

Joshua sighed and closed his eyes. Why did his father hate him so much? "The woman doesn't want me. She thinks I'm a bug under her boot. Why won't my father leave me alone?"

The cowhand brushed away his concerns with an innocent gaze. "I got no thoughts on the business. My job's taking your hide to the courthouse on time. Judge is awaiting. Your pa said your bride will be there after your ma fixes her up right and proper. The belle of ball… that's the lady. But if you ask me, she's on the skinny side. Better add some meat to her bones after the wedding."

Joshua sat up with a sense of doom plaguing his heels. He wondered if his father had lost his sense of reason. "She's dressed?" A quick glance at the clock showed the time, and he shook his head. "It's eight-o-clock. How can she be dressed?"

The cowhand tipped his hat and nodded with a twist of his lips. "That's not my place to say, but she's mighty fair—blushing, too. Now get a move on, sir. I'd sure hate to shoot you on your wedding day."

Joshua groaned and prayed for patience. Despite the less-than-stellar offer, the cowhand had a mean streak a mile wide when crossed. Joshua didn't doubt he might empty the entire six-shot revolver if called to arms. With a frustrated groan that burned his gut, he jumped off the bed. Time to join in the holy bonds of matrimony—or else.

An idea came to him between putting on his boots and his pants, and Joshua froze. A plan formed and gained momentum by the time he curled his bow tie's knot. Time to show his father and his future wife that things weren't always what they appeared to be. *Miss Barrington, you can lead a horse to the water, but you can't make him drink.*

Mrs. Joshua Wallace. Willow tested the title on her lips and found it strange. Events raced by in a blur, leaving her little time to think, and now her husband stood beside her with a stoic face wrapped in a cloud of silence.

That same night, they left the Wallace family home in a covered buggy with glass bottles and wreaths tumbling behind the wheels. Willow didn't understand the rush to leave, but she held her tongue; she had caused enough damage by insulting Joshua's honor, and she regretted it.

When a boulder in the road caused the buggy to lurch, Willow lost her seating and crashed against her husband. She murmured a breathless apology and scrambled over to the side, careful to adjust her lace skirt. Her words collided with a brick wall of silence; Joshua didn't flinch or even turn his head. He fixed his gaze on the road and said nothing.

Dismayed at the lack of reaction Willow tried to make peace, conscious of the earlier blunder. Unwilling to let the matter drop, she said, "I'm so sorry."

He started in surprise and murmured. "What? Oh —didn't mean to ignore you. Caught up in crazy thoughts."

Joshua's absentminded response induced a wave of relief and a sigh whispered past Willow's lips. Thankful the first marital hurdle was past, she wondered how far the cabin stood. She couldn't help but notice how the moonless night obscured the clumps of greenery and engulfed the plains in a mantle of darkness. Thankful that the horses knew their way in the shadows, she shivered.

"Wind's too brisk? You'll find a blanket under the seat."

Touched at the solicitous observation, she replied, "Thank you. The wind is fresh and smells glorious. Reminds me of green meadows, wild flowers and endless pastures."

Joshua chuckled at the comment as though tickled by her sense of wonder.

Willow loved the cheerful sound and wondered how his chest might rumble against her cheek. Stunned at how much she desired his powerful embrace, she peered into the darkness. She knew her face and neck were flushed, but she felt so different. *Willow Barrington. Aren't you a spinster at heart?*

"Yes, it's nice out here and much nicer by the cabin. We'll explore the area together in the next few days."

Willow appreciated the ease of his offer, but something troubled her. Careful to keep her words even, she wondered out loud, "Joshua, I don't mean to pry and please don't be angry, but I have a question to ask."

"Shoot."

Willow blinked and grinned. He had such a way with words. "Your father told me you didn't plan to marry. Will our marriage be a tremendous burden to your plans?"

He paused at the tentative question and remained silent for a few moments. Then his answer came with a hint of regret, "I learned of your problem after I spoke to you last night. Hope you can forgive my overbearing manners."

Willow touched his sinewy arm and pulled back in haste when his muscles flexed. Did he want her to touch him or not? Better stick to forgiveness for now. "Your words mean so much."

She couldn't see his wide smile in response, but she sensed it. When she snuggled next to his solid frame, he didn't pull away. Content, she allowed the warmth of his body to warm her own.

I wonder what tomorrow will bring?

CHAPTER 9

SOMETHING WET PLANTED A WINTER'S KISS ON HER cheek, and Willow stirred. When she opened gritty eyes and caught sight of the snow-white beast in her room, she buried a scream and pinched her eyes shut.

The massive animal stood next to her pillow, his warm breath caressing her cheek. After a few minutes, Willow opened her eyes and gazed into the hazel orbs. The wolf mewled and wagged his tail. When he placed a large paw on her stomach, Willow held her breath.

He continued to watch her with unblinking intensity and lowered his head. When she touched his fur with a tender hand, he lay next to the bed.

Willow grinned and released a pent-up breath.

"Why, you're nothing but a big old softy," she said as she stroked his coat. "Sorry, my friend, but I have to get out of bed now."

The opened window let in the morning light. Willow turned to look at the faint outline of evergreen trees grouped together in the distance. The glare of the morning sun hit her dead in the face, and her bones stirred. When she covered her eyes with her left hand, the gleam of a golden band around her ring finger caught her eye. Mrs. Joshua Wallace. How strange to be married when she'd planned to stay a spinster.

She hurried off the bed and stood on the frigid floor. Why didn't she remember arriving at the cabin? Had she been that tired or asleep? What happened to their wedding night?

Ashamed at her giant lapse in memory, Willow hurried to wash and get dressed. A large tub rusted with age stood in the corner of the barren room. No other furnishings were in the room, except for a bureau with her carryall on top, and a large bed that dominated the interior. Next to the tub stood a moss-covered bucket filled with crystalline water and a kettle.

Willow found a simple summer frock to wear and yanked it over her head. Running Deer, Joshua's mother, had promised to send other clothing along with shoes and ribbons. Willow sensed her mother-in-law's affection, and responded in kind. She hoped to see her again soon, even if the house stood at a distance from the town, more than an hour's journey.

After she was ready, she took a moment to make the bed. It was then that she noticed the imprint on the cotton sheets was her own; where had Joshua spent the night?

Willow didn't have time to ponder the issue, because when she opened the bedroom door, she met five pairs of curious eyes. Shocked to see a bedraggled group of children with dirty faces and unwashed bodies, Willow wondered if she was still asleep. She moved toward the kitchen and the group followed close behind her steps.

"She's a girl," the smallest one piped up, as though stunned at the thought.

The largest of the group sneered at the innocent comment and said, "Yeah, she's a girl. Boss man said he was bringing a squaw for a wife, but she ain't no squaw. She's one of them schoolteachers that thrash you when you don't say your sums right."

The other boys agreed and crowded at Willow's

side. They tugged at her dress and poked her in the stomach with guttural grunts.

Willow bore their poking with a smile, but when they danced in a haphazard circle and howled, she decided enough was enough. "Children, please stop at once."

When they came to a standstill, she lowered herself to one knee and faced them. They were of similar height, with tanned skin, dark eyes, and dark hair. "Now, be so kind as to give your names, and watch your manners when you do."

When they stared at her with gaping mouths, she repeated herself. "Give me your names, please."

"They don't have familiar names, so I gave them numbers. Boys, pay your respects to the lady of the house."

Joshua blocked the doorway with his tall frame. A rested look and a clean-shaven face caught Willow off guard and sent her senses in a scramble. The intensity of his gaze pierced her soul and whipped her heart into thunderous beats.

Shaken by the powerful emotion, she turned back to the children to hide the flush on her face. "Well, I want to hear their names, no matter how difficult, if they don't mind sharing them with me."

To Willow's surprise, the boys lined up by order

of height. One by one, they introduced themselves in singsong voices. Flying Eagle, Swift Horse, Running Wolf, Snow Owl, and Black Fox.

Touched at their acceptance after Joshua's words, Willow hugged them and planted soft kisses on the tops of their heads. When they yelled in cheerful unison and raced outdoors, Willow's heart tugged in response. The first shock had faded, and in customary fashion, she made the best of things.

The children needed care, and if Joshua wanted to help, she planned to support the decision. When she spied his cheerful gaze, Willow murmured. "Are they from around here?"

He nodded and ambled over to the half-built cupboard, removing grubby plates and chipped glasses. "Yeah. A reservation in the neighborhood, a couple miles away. Think they ran away, but never asked. We sleep in a shed around the back of the house and share a bunk. I plan to build more rooms when I fix the cabin, but haven't done it yet." He paused briefly, and then looked at her with pleading eyes, "Please, Willow… don't ask me to return them to the reservation. These kids mean everything to me."

Willow's mind turned in circles. Did she want to

take young boys under her care? What if things didn't work out? What if they hated her?

A sense of right flowed through her veins and she stepped back. The boys and Joshua needed her help. In customary Barrington fashion, she squared her shoulders and tilted her chin. She'd raised two sisters, so five boys shouldn't be that hard. "I'd never ask that. If you want to keep them, I will support your decision."

When a relieved grin flashed, deepening the grooves in his splendid cheeks, Willow smiled in response. "I will get the boys to show me the lay of the land. Do you think they will enjoy doing that?"

Joshua nodded and then his smile grew wry. "Sure. But if they tie you to a tree don't say I didn't warn you."

Willow ignored the mischievous glint in his eye and placed her hands on her slender hips. "Not to worry. I can hold my own."

He arched a brow and whistled. "Yes, Ma'am. I'm sure you can."

JOSHUA RECLINED ON A BRANCH AND GAZED AT THE sun dipping behind the mountain peaks. When it sank beneath the horizon, fiery threads leaped across the expanse as though begging for the molten orb's return. A heavy darkness enveloped the land and the first twinkles of starlight dotted the sky. *Time to head back.*

He sighed and turned toward the house in the distance watching the lights flickering in the windows. It had been one month since he and Willow became man and wife, and somewhere along the line she had become indispensable to him.

The first thing she had done was clean the entire cabin, leaving it spotless. Joshua marveled at the color of the wood he hadn't seen in ages due to grime. He admitted he had been a poor housekeeper.

Then she scrubbed the floor until it resembled polished oak. That surprised him even more. Who knew he had such beautiful wood under his feet? She fed the boys on time, made them clothing, and read them stories from the Bible. When they clamored for her attention, she taught them with a kind spirit to recognize their gifts and virtues. Her winsome but firm personality led Joshua to believe an angel had descended to his doorstep.

Joshua wanted to share his burgeoning feelings with his wife, but he wanted to do it in a special way. After washing at the edge of the stream, an idea brewed in his mind. He planned to go to town and get a special gift.

He shuddered at his decision and smiled. *Joshua Wallace, you are in danger of losing your heart.*

CHAPTER 11

WILLOW HUMMED A CHEERFUL TUNE AND WONDERED why the boys had fallen silent. She needed to check on them, but wanted to do something first.

Joshua had gone to Riverside for the day, with a promise to take her the following week. Willow appreciated his offer, and hurried to write a letter to her sisters.

She knew her husband struggled to make a life for them both on the vast plains and she respected his choice. But Horton, Joshua's father, had promised to send money to care for her parents and help pay the bank. Grateful for his kindness, Willow had accepted and shared the good news with her sisters.

As she penned her experiences over the past

month, Willow paused and wondered how to share her innermost feelings. One of the most important things she had realized was how much her marriage to Joshua affected her. When she spoke to him, she lingered in a daze, caught in a world where only the impact of their eyes anchored them in place.

Sometimes, when he looked at her, she held her breath, hoping he might say he loved her. But when he kept silent, she dismissed it as fanciful longing on her part.

Being lost in her thoughts left Willow unprepared for the terrified cries of her name. She stumbled to her feet and raced to the door with a thudding heart and breathless prayers. *Dear Lord, is that the boys?*

When she got outside, the piercing light of the morning sun blinded her for an instant. When the hazy outline of riders came into view, she screamed in fear. A roughshod group of men with narrow eyes and holstered guns scooped up the boys and rode away in a cloud of prairie dust. She raced behind them in fruitless pursuit but a man—dressed in a fine suit with a balding head and oversized glasses —crossed her path.

He thrust a piece of white paper in her flushed

face and said, "My name is Miles Cowell, and those orphans are wanted back on the reservation."

Willow struggled to catch her breath, her lungs on fire. She peered into the distance, trying to follow the path of the men. The riders had long gone, and the boys with them, leaving only a faint trail behind them. She held the paper in her bloodless hands and scanned the note with frantic eyes. "But… sir, my husband cares for the boys and they…. they want to stay with us."

Mr. Cowell flicked an invisible piece of lint from his tailored suit, and his eyes gleamed with disdain. "I do not believe your husband can care for you, much less these children. Tell Mr. Wallace that I said the next time he plans to encourage misbehavior, he should have a child of his own."

Willow gasped at the harsh words and wondered why the man disliked Joshua. It didn't take long for him to make his position understood.

"The Wallaces of this county need to understand that money doesn't buy everything. There are laws and rules to follow, Missy, and your husband had better understand that."

Willow's stomach twisted into knots and she moistened her dry lips. Trying to defuse the tension in the air, she countered his claim but remained respectful. "My husband is not wealthy, sir. He knows he can't step above the laws of the land."

Mr. Cowell laughed. The sound reeked of contempt. "Nonsense. Old Man Wallace? He'd give his children the moon if he could. You should know that by now." Then his eyes raked over her slim frame, stripping her to the bone, and his lips curled, "I am sure you will enjoy his 'generosity' soon."

Willow recoiled at the virulent spite and intent. She didn't know why this man held such a deep-seated dislike for Joshua's family, and she didn't care. A wave of protective instinct flooded her heart, and she stepped forward and tilted her chin up. Mr. Cowell might be an officer of the county, but that didn't give him the right to sully her husband's name or disparage her in such a way.

"Mr. Cowell, you are not a gentleman. My husband belongs to one of the most upstanding families in this county, and I bear his name. I don't know the judges here, but I will drive into town and find one. Please remove yourself from our land and try to make sure that *my* children are not harmed. If you do not see to their safety, I will see you fired from any position I daresay you scraped the barrel to get."

Unwilling to apologize for her words or take

them back, Willow raced back to her house. She had to get to town, and Joshua had ridden his horse, which left the buggy at her disposal. The precise mechanics of the contraption eluded her, but it was a great day to learn.

CHAPTER 12

"MR. WALLACE. SIR, PLEASE COME. TROUBLE'S A-coming."

The maid's frantic voice spurred Joshua to the front porch. He watched the buggy tear a hole across the street, the wheels spitting up pellets and mud. Gigantic puffs of dust rose in a swirling cloud as it picked up speed, scattering pedestrians along the way. When it appeared to race past the house, the driver stopped the horse with a firm command. The buggy jarred to a shuddered halt, and the occupant leaped from the seat.

When the driver raced toward the house, Joshua did a double take and blinked. Who was the frazzle haired woman with flushed cheeks and wild eyes?

When Willow launched herself into his arms

with a heartfelt sob, he embraced her with a lopsided grin. Had she missed him that much? It had been less than a day.

When her tears lessened, Joshua's face split into a wide, toothy grin. He wanted to share with Willow how much she meant to him, and join their lives as one. His thoughts lingered in blissful union until her words tore them from his mind.

"Joshua… the children are gone. A horrible man showed up… and carried them away."

Joshua's heart stilled, and a roar rushed through his ears. He disentangled himself and raised her chin to look into her tear-filled eyes. Careful to keep his voice even, he asked, "Who took the children? When?"

"It happened after you left. A horrid man called Miles Cowell... he came and said horrible things. Then he took the children."

Joshua sucked in a deep breath, his mind racing over scenarios—none of them good.

Cowell. The thorn in his family's flesh. Dismissing thoughts of his disgruntled neighbor, Joshua turned to the matter at hand. "Judge Faraday is by the courthouse. He will give me the permission I need. He's a family friend, and I'm sure he will help. The reservation is not that far away."

At the frantic concern in her eyes, he drew her back into his embrace and placed his cheek next to her own. "Don't worry. I will get them back. You stay here with my parents and get something to eat."

"Yes, darling."

Joshua's heart stilled mid-beat. *Darling. Did she say that? The children, Joshua. Remember the children.* "Uh, that's wonderful, Willow. Um, we will discuss this later, but please don't forget what you said. Be right back."

Joshua's strides ate up the ground, but with each step, Willow's words beat in the back of his mind. *Yes, darling.* She cared for him, and it filled him with elation. Then his thoughts betrayed him with a stab of doubt; did she care, or were they only words?

CHAPTER 13

JUDGE FARADAY PROVED HELPFUL, AND JOSHUA GOT the permission he needed. Miles Cowell sneered when he entered the reservation, but Joshua ignored him. As long as he had the judge's permission, Miles could do nothing or stop him from taking the boys.

When they caught sight of him, they crowded his legs, trying to climb up at the same time. Joshua grinned and said, "Whoa now there, partners. I can tell you're mighty glad to see me. Don't think I've ever seen you so eager."

Black Fox said, "We want our mama. She feeds us and tells us nice stories. We will be good boys so she can stay."

Swift Horse agreed with a gap-toothed smile. "Yes, and you better be good. We'll watch you too."

50

Joshua nodded. "Mama is waiting for you and she's planned a real nice supper, with apple pie for dessert."

The boys cheered in unison, and Joshua ruffled their heads and whispered a prayer of thanks.

The boys devoured supper, much to Willow's delight. She watched them eat with moist eyes and hurried to find Joshua. He reclined on the porch swing and watched the evening lights creep lower in the horizon.

When he caught sight of her, he waved her to his side. "The judge admitted I need special permission to keep them, so I need to get it done. And I need a bigger house. The truth is they can't stay in the shed much longer, so I asked my father for help. But I am not taking charity. I plan to work hard and pay back every cent. Will you help me?"

Touched to hear his wish for her help, Willow's heart melted into a puddle at her feet. She admired his independence and his modest spirit. "I'd be honored. Don't you know I made a vow before heaven to stand by your side no matter what happens?"

Joshua drew her close and cradled her head next to his heart. "You called me darling earlier today. Did you mean it?"

She chuckled against his chest. "Of course, I meant it. I love you, Joshua, and I'll say it again, too, if you don't mind."

He sucked in a deep breath and raised her chin to stare into her eyes. Their gazes locked and held. "I love you too, Willow, and you can say it as often as you want. I will never tire of hearing it." Tears pooled in Willow's eyes and she murmured, "Then I will never tire of saying it."

Joshua nodded and pulled her closer. Content, they sat for a while admiring the billowing clouds in the distance and how the shadows played with the light.

"My darling, something slipped my mind. Your brother Jasper told me you are a fool for settling into married life. I gather he doesn't intend to follow in your footsteps."

Joshua shook his head. "He's just rotten." When Willow gave him a look, he rushed to amend his words. "Not too rotten, but we'll discuss it another day. Let's mosey on home. We have a house to build and five boys to fill up the space. We might even have a few boys of our own if you're willing." He smiled, "Guess we should throw in a few girls, too; turns out I like women more than I thought."

Willow gasped in delight. She threw her arms around his neck and placed a soft kiss on his lips. She felt humbled and blessed to have found such a kind and loving husband to share her life with. "Yes, Darling," she chuckled. "Let's 'mosey' on home."

EPILOGUE

HORTON OBSERVED JOSHUA AND WILLOW WITH A WIDE smile from behind the slit in the curtain. He clapped his hands when they kissed, and whistled under his breath.

Running Deer watched him eavesdrop in shameless fashion, and poked him in the side. "Will you stop that? Give them a moment alone and come help me. Those boys are ripping a hole in the floor."

Horton had no time for such trivial pursuits, and ignored the summons. "Not now, woman. My mind's churning up a plan. You know how many problems Jasper is giving us because he won't get his head out of the clouds. Willow has two more sisters, and Eliza Walkerton told me that Lily was the perfect choice for him. How's that for a plan, eh?"

Running Deer eyed him with a frustrated glance and crossed her arms. "Stop matchmaking, and don't you even think of leading another one of our sons to the altar at gunpoint. I still haven't forgiven you for that."

Horton placed his hands in the shape of a steeple under his chin and lowered his head. "Yes, dear. I promise."

When she departed, he turned back to the window, and a mysterious smile clung to the edge of his lips. *Lily, my dear, fancy a trip out west?*

THE END

MAIL ORDER BRIDE LILY

BRIDES OF RIVERSIDE

CHAPTER 1

BATH, MAINE. JUNE, 1896.

LILY SQUEALED IN DELIGHT AND HURRIED TO THE drawing room, her mind a jumble of anticipation. A cup of fragrant tea and a plate of honey biscuits lay on the side table, but she ignored the evening ritual. The words of the letter held her rapt attention, and she remained engrossed in the scribbled content.

...DID I tell you the house is done? I have enough space for everyone and I know you will love it here. My father-in-law will put you up for a few days, and I'll make the trip out as soon as I can; you know I need to care for the boys. But, please come now, Dearest. I miss you.

With love,
Willow

LILY'S HEART raced a mile a minute. She longed for a journey and excitement. Something new and thrilling. And now, she held the opportunity in her hands. *Thank you, dearest sister.*

A frisson of fear replaced anticipation. The letter begged her to come to California in two weeks. *Two weeks.* Lily's stomach twisted into knots and the muscles tightened; she'd never traveled alone before, and wondered if the road was safe.

Who knew what dangers lay in the wild expanse engulfed in miles of ever-changing sand? What if highwaymen ambushed the train? Or masked cowboys whipped up a gunfight among unsuspecting passengers? Didn't wild Indians roam the hills on surefooted horses?

According to Willow, California boasted a vivid landscape full of hope and wonder. Lily felt sure her sister exaggerated the delights, but there might be redeemable attributes. The letter spoke of happiness, and the contentment of a new home. *Happily ever after in one lassoed bundle.* Could it be true?

Lily turned to the faint charcoal embers behind

the grate. The blazing fire had long died and a warm glow simmered. She wondered if her life might whip up into endless flames someday, or languish in nonentity.

She'd planned to attract a handsome suitor with a heart of gold, but knew the chances were slim. No dowry and nigh a penny to the Barrington name enticed few gentlemen. And it meant few party invitations to reputable venues where gentlemen flocked in search of a bride. How could she find Prince Charming if she couldn't get to the ball? *Fairy godmother, where are you?*

Lily thought of Willow. It had only been a year since she'd left to become Joshua Wallace's mail-order bride. The marriage contract brought five orphans with the package, but Willow embraced the change with a full heart. Lily admired the decision and wondered if she could do the same. *Dear Lord, please guide my steps.*

"Lily! I'm home."

Rose had arrived. Lily clutched the letter and considered her choices. Stay and die an old maid, or see what surprises California held?

CHAPTER 2

"You plan to travel… by *yourself*?"

Rose's incredulous tone lashed Lily's waning courage, but she brushed off the distrustful note and did the best to keep a stiff upper lip. Willow said it helped keep a person's courage to the fore. "Yes, I am going by myself. Just because you're the youngest doesn't mean you're the only brave one in the family."

Rose rolled her eyes and made a face, and Lily continued, "The moment I get there, Horton Wallace will pick me up and take me to the house. I am to spend just a couple nights and Willow will come to fetch me later. She's busy with the orphans, but she said I will be just fine at the Wallace home."

Rose arched a brow at the breathless timbre and

interpreted Lily's strained face with ease. "Lily, you can't even walk to the corner without being fearful, and you burst into tears at the sight of a stray dog. I think we'd better make plans to travel together. There is enough money to cover both of our tickets, even though I planned to travel later."

Lily's chin took on a stubborn tilt, and she crossed her arms. Despite her intense wish for companionship, she wanted her sibling to see her bravery. "There's no need to come. I can find my way. Leave me at the station and I will board the train, then Horton Wallace will pick me up when I arrive. It is as simple as a cup of elderberry tea."

Rose turned to Lily with a wry grin. "Well, if your decision is to go alone, I respect that. You might even meet a handsome beau and get married. Think of happily ever after, dearest sister."

Lily squealed at the thought. *Happily ever after?* That only happened in fairytales. The idea held frank appeal, then she sobered at her lack of finances. "I doubt it. No man wants a poor waif with nothing to offer the marriage table—not even in California."

CHAPTER 3

RIVERSIDE, CALIFORNIA

"When are you going to behave, boy? This is the third time the marshal's been here. I have told you, this wild behavior must stop."

Jasper roused from a deep slumber at the sound of his father's voice. The light of the lamp reached him and he groaned. He rubbed his grit-filled eyes and smothered a colossal yawn. He shifted his muscular frame, semi-covered by a snow-white sheet, and flexed his taut shoulders. What did the old man want? And why did he wake him?

When blurred hazel eyes collided with a heated glare, Jasper sat up and flashed a rakish grin. Better douse the air before things flamed hotter than the desert sand. "Everything good, Pa?"

Horton grunted and shook his head. "No. Everything is not *good*."

Jasper scrambled for a good excuse but nothing surfaced. "Pa, whatever they said I done, I didn't do," he muttered.

Horton's eyes glinted and his expression smoldered. "Didn't you?"

Jasper scratched his head. He tried to organize his thoughts and glanced at the wall clock. Not even the melodious chirp of morning birds stirred, and the sun still dipped below the horizon. Might have to organize his thoughts later. He arranged the feathered pillows against the wooden headboard and winced at the sharp pain that struck his back.

His father's molten gaze missed nothing, and he nodded.

"Sore, eh? Serves you right. The marshal told me you and the boys tore up the street. Must've thought you were wild buckaroos galloping through town. I told you those horses are for auction and not for a stuffed-shirt dandy."

Jasper gawked and wondered where his father got the term 'stuffed-shirt dandy;' must be from those books he loved to read. As Horton continued his reprimand, Jasper's thoughts trailed to other matters.

He fingered the stubble on his angular jaw and decided a shave might be in order. Daisy May expected him to take her out for dinner in the evening, and she despised a shaded chin—then again, Daisy May despised *most* things.

When his father stopped talking, Jasper hurried to offer more paltry excuses. "Nothing happened, Pa. There's no need to get upset. I'll apologize to the marshal this morning."

Horton blasted his youngest son with a fiery frown and stepped back. "You'll do that later. Right now, I need your services at the train. Lily Barrington is coming this morning, and I want you to pick her up at the station."

Jasper racked the vacuum in his brain. *Lily Barrington?* The name brought no memories of past dalliances or forbidden sweethearts. "Who's Lily?"

Horton shook his head and rolled his eyes. "My star's boy. Your brother Joshua is married to her sister Willow. Don't you remember her speaking of Lily and Rose? They're her sisters, from back east."

Jasper shrugged and examined his low-cut nails. "Nope. Don't remember a thing. Send a worker to get her. The train is never on time. Besides, I'm going out with Daisy for dinner."

"The sun has addled your brain and cooked what's left of your good sense."

Jasper started in surprise at the implacable steel in his father's voice. It brooked no disobedience to his plans. "Pa, is there a special reason you want me to pick her up from the train?"

Horton ambled over to the wide-framed window and stared off into the distance. An air of stillness clung to him, and his strong shoulders blocked out the budding light of dawn. "I've been thinking it's time for you to plant roots and start a family."

Jasper sat up in shock and drew a harsh breath. He swallowed a mountain-sized lump and wondered if he had fallen back asleep. *Plant roots and start a family?* Heck no!

Thinking his father must have an urgent reason for such harsh words, Jasper asked, "Pa, is Ma sick... or are you?"

The reply mingled with a deep sigh. "No, we're fine, but here's the plan son: your days of hard-headed behavior have ended. You've had no responsibilities or felt the need, and I let it slip. It's my fault and I accept that, but there's still time to fix my mistakes. Do you understand?"

Jasper wondered if he needed to fetch the doctor. "Um, okay Pa. But why do you want me to meet Lily Barrington?"

Horton smiled with his mouth but not with his eyes. Alarm bells raced through Jasper's mind just before his father said the words he never expected to hear.

"I've decided she'll make the perfect bride."

Daisy May Meriwether blossomed in a layered pink dress with silver ruffles and endless ribbons. Vibrant chestnut waves lay tamed in an elegant bun encircled with fragrant daisies. As she turned, the sunlight created a copper halo that illuminated the curve of her soft cheeks and swanlike neck. Many beaus had lost their heart at her dainty feet.

Daisy May loved Riverside, and her family invested in the citrus trade, which lent a lucrative flair to the Meriwether Empire. The spacious three-story home flourished under the care of Daisy's parents, who never lost a moment to offer the liveliest entertainment and the tastiest food.

When Jasper appeared at her porch steps, Daisy

May's emerald eyes sparkled. The wraparound clapboard porch with its decorative trim provided a splendid backdrop as she rushed to embrace him. She planted a butterfly kiss on his cheek and fluttered long lashes. "So nice to see you. Come visit for a spell."

He returned her affectionate greeting with an absentminded murmur and eased into the open arms of the curved porch swing.

"I'm surprised to see you so soon. I thought you were taking me for dinner this evening."

At Jasper's disgruntled expression, Daisy's delicate brow puckered. "Oh my. Why such a frown?"

"My Pa."

Daisy started in surprise. She knew Horton was a good father, doting on his sons. Jasper never had cause to complain, but he'd never spoken to her in such a brusque manner. "Tell me what's wrong. Maybe I can help."

"My father wants me to marry a girl from the east."

Daisy stared at Jasper as if he'd plucked a buffalo out of thin air. His words filled her with dread and she scrambled for a witty response. "You must have hit your head yesterday when you rode across town."

He tossed her a wry glance and shook his head. "I'm not that far gone, and you heard me. A girl by the name of Lily Barrington is coming today, and I have to pick her up at the station."

Daisy's mind raced, branching in multiple directions. Jasper belonged to her, and no one, much less a simpleton from the east, could have him.

Careful not to spook the fragile trust she'd earned over the past few months, she calmed her nerves. It took every ounce of control she possessed to keep her tone even. "Your Pa must've lost his head in a poker game, but I think have a way to help you with your problem."

At his raised brow, she hurried to explain. "Go to the station and meet her. Be tender and kind, at first, but then treat her as a leech. Your Pa will have no choice but to send her packing."

Jasper's look of admiration flattered Daisy's vanity, and she lowered her lids to hide her tenacious gaze.

"Gracious, Miss Meriwether. I wonder if your father knows what's brewing under his roof. Seems a little harsh, don't you think?"

Daisy struggled to stay calm and struck a nonchalant pose. "I understand, but please listen. If you do what I say, she will leave and then you will get your freedom back."

Jasper chewed on the thought for a moment, then a wide, mischievous grin splashed across his face, outlining the grooves in his cheeks.

CHAPTER 5

THE SOUTHERN PACIFIC TRAIN SCREECHED TO A belching halt, drenched in gigantic plumes of smoke under a diaphanous sky. When the puffs cleared, Lily's wide eyes drank in the scene.

Gilded plains mixed with verdant patches and tall trees rose to meet her. She thought of the grandeur spread before her and thought of a banquet table with exotic meals. In her wildest dreams, she had never imagined a land bathed in golden sunlight.

Quick steps took her off the steel car. She swung her carryall in cramped hands, and bit back a groan at the vigorous action. Her purse strings did not extend to the comforts of a Pullman carriage, and the trip had taken its toll. Her bones interlocked under a sore back, but she bore the discomfort without a murmur.

When she got off the train and stepped across the rails, delicious warmth enveloped her. She breathed in the scented air and smiled; it smelled fresh and full of promise.

The surroundings swirled in bursts of excited chatter as passengers surged back and forth. Lily did her best to get her bearings and moved with the crowd over uneven rails and dust-filled tracks. The one-floor station with a passenger platform stood as a solemn beacon, but Lily preferred the majestic outdoors.

She craned her neck to find a porter to ask for directions, and a voice spoke over her shoulder.

"Miss Barrington? Lily?"

The deep rumble reverberated around her, and Lily froze. When she turned, her eyes widened at the tall, good-looking stranger with a russet gaze. He wore his attire well, and it suited his muscular frame. Silence pounded in her ears and Lily struggled to find her tongue.

"Yes, my name is Lily Barrington."

His eyes fell to the tattered carryall, and he plucked it out of her hands. "Jasper Wallace, son of

Horton Wallace, at your esteemed service. Please follow me, Miss."

Lily watched his powerful shoulders and confident strides blend into the parting crowd. She hesitated. Willow had sent a picture of her husband Joshua, and the resemblance to the Wallace family was undeniable. At least he wasn't a highwayman or robber. Lily cringed at her wild imagination and bit her inner cheek. *Stop your wild fancies!*

"Today, Miss Barrington."

His impatient call spurred her forward, and Lily bristled. She thought people of the West were supposed to have friendlier personalities, but then she groaned and chided herself. *Judge not lest ye be judged.*

She stumbled across the platform and spied his wrinkled frown when she got to the end. When he helped her into the one-horse buggy, she arranged her dress and kept silent. They drove off in a dust-filled blur, and Lily wondered what she had done to inspire such a frown.

She's not what I imagined. Jasper struggled to get his thoughts back on track, and wondered why he felt out of sorts. To give himself time to come to terms with his newfound emotions, he kept an easy speed and allowed his guest to drink in the view.

The seasons of Riverside boasted an ever-changing canvas below cerulean skies and silvery clouds. In place of molten plains, burnt grass, and little rain, Riverside basked in winter's dew, summer breezes and spring rain.

The town bustled as a temperance-minded neighbor to San Bernardino, and found its place among valleys and gentle, sloping hills. It had solid Republican folks, and no saloons to disturb the peace. Countless Revival-style homes dotted the scenic landscape with well-kept gardens, low fences, and pristine walkways.

"I love it. You are blessed to live in a fertile place. On the way here, I noticed a fair amount of brown sand, barren plains, and very few trees."

Lily's soft-spoken voice carried on the morning wind and tingled Jasper's ear. He grunted at her comment and agreed in his mind. When he first saw her, he thought she was far too thin and lackluster for his taste. She had little in the way of a curvaceous figure, and her hair fell in drab lines—or at least the lines he could see tucked under her bonnet. But the lack of these attributes paled in comparison to the excitement on her heart-shaped face.

Her childlike glow was contagious. The joy that colored her cheeks resembled the moist petals of the

MAIL ORDER BRIDE LILY

morning rose. Her curiosity and sense of enchant-
ment touched him. This was troubling, and he didn't
understand why he should care, so his thoughts
returned to the plan he'd discussed with Daisy May:
treat her as a leech.

When Lily craned her body and neck to an
impossible degree, he wondered how she kept her
balance. The comical sight filled him with laughter.
"You'll tumble out if you don't watch yourself."

She whirled with a muffled yelp and blinked.
"Sorry. Too much excitement, I suppose. It's so
colorful here, Mr. Wallace! Tell me, what are those
trees?"

He followed her gaze and explained, "Those are
Bahia trees. Navel oranges. My family is part of this
industry. Got a big plantation out of town. In the
town itself, you will see rows and rows of the trees
everywhere."

"Your father must be happy to have your help
with such important work."

The statement struck Jasper on an odd note.
Until that moment, he had never considered
joining the family business. "I don't work with my
father."

"Oh." The tone carried an implied question, and
he felt obliged to respond.

77

"He doesn't want a stuffed shirt dandy helping him, I'm sure."

She shook her head and blessed him with a heartfelt smile. "Nonsense. I am sure your father will be happy with your help. My sister Willow tells me it only takes a willing spirit. And the Bible taught me that anything is possible if you have faith."

Jasper avoided an oncoming wagon with a family of four. *She reads the Bible? Daisy May doesn't even do that.* "Makes sense, I suppose."

When she turned back to the scenery, he scratched his head in wonder. There was more to Lily Barrington than met the eye. And he wanted to know more.

CHAPTER 6

"You did *what*?"

Daisy May's heart hammered in painful thumps. She shot Jasper a tight glance and directed him to the family parlor. Among the rustic furniture with carved oak handles and bright cushions, she examined his troubled face.

One flick of her wrist brought a solemn servant in pristine attire, and Daisy ordered refreshments. She pinned Jasper with a glare and demanded, "Explain how the plan went wrong. What did you do?"

He shrugged and replied, "She isn't a terrible person. You should see how she gawks at everything with her saucer eyes. My mother loves her."

Daisy shuddered at the curious note. Something

had changed. Jasper appeared intrigued instead of offended. Curious instead of insulted.

She buried the virulent spite that clogged her veins and kept her innermost feelings in check. "Treat her as a leech, remember? What happened to the plan we discussed?"

Jasper threw back his head and glanced at the ceiling. He appeared fascinated with the laced pattern and intricate paneled design. "She wears her heart on her sleeve and cries at the drop of a spur. When she met my Pa, she sobbed all over him. Reminded me of a water trough."

Daisy rose on shaking legs and wondered at the admiration in Jasper's voice. Did he want her to whip up tears out of the blue? She knew how to keep her composure in polite company. "You will just have to try again. I am guessing your Pa is having a big feast tonight. Just ignore her. That can't be too hard, right?"

Jasper closed his eyes and muttered, "Not sure. She can be hard to ignore."

Daisy crushed her frustration and thanked her parents for her iron will. She recognized the danger of Jasper's absentminded behavior, and her mind raced. Lost after one meeting? How was that possible?

If Jasper held fascination for the Barrington girl, he'd abandon Daisy on the spot. She couldn't bear the thought. He was the only person she talked to—her only friend—and she planned to join their families together by becoming his wife. Surely no Easterner could thwart her plan.

Daisy took a deep breath and planted a come-hither look on her face. Her lashes fanned her cheeks, and she pouted. "Jasper, I am shocked at you. Can't you do this one little thing for me?"

He turned to her in surprise. "I'm always doing things for you. Stop mumbling over nothing."

Daisy gritted her teeth under a tight smile. The dense nature of men's thoughts could be impossible to understand. "Just ignore her for a few days. Your father will think you're not suitable. That will end the arrangement, and you'll be free again."

Jasper considered her plan, then he agreed with reluctance. "Okay, guess I can try. Now stop beating my ear to pieces and get me something to eat. I'm starved."

Daisy released a pent-up breath and her shoulders sagged in relief. *Whatever you say, darling.*

CHAPTER 7

LILY TWIRLED IN HER PRIMROSE DRESS BEFORE THE gilded frame mirror. It enhanced the curve of her waist and the highlights in her eyes. She hurried to finish dressing and arranged her hair in an elegant bun, then gathered her writing supplies together to send a letter to her sisters in Maine.

She couldn't help but marvel at how much things had changed in one week. First, Willow couldn't make the trip. Two of the orphans got sick with fever, and that kept her busy with their care. She had sent word to say she'd make the trip as soon as she could. This gave Lily the opportunity to consider her future; uppermost in her mind was Horton's offer.

She had had a private meeting with the elder Wallace two nights after her arrival. He'd invited her to his study and laid out his plan with practical efficiency.

If it wasn't for the flicker of pain in his eyes, Lily might have dismissed his words. As it was, she felt sorry for him, and wanted to show how much she appreciated his trust.

When they had met, he had spoken in a low, steady voice. At the forefront of his mind was his son's future, and he shared his concerns with his guest.

"Jasper needs help. He's a wastrel without a care in the world, sad as the words might sound. His best friend is Daisy May Meriwether. She's not the woman for him, and she'll never be. Always up to her neck in trouble and getting away with things by the skin of her teeth. I think she feels Jasper is a kindred spirit and gets him into more trouble than I can count. A stable life is what he needs—a solid home and a fine woman. Can you help me?"

Lily remembered silence and scattered thoughts. At first, she thought it was a cruel joke, and then she saw the depths of emotion in his gaze. "Mr. Wallace, I came to visit my sister, not to get married."

Horton had brushed off her concerns with a wave. "Willow is the most levelheaded girl I know, and you're her sister. You can help my son to become a better man. To have a sense of responsibility."

When Lily stayed silent, Horton sighed. He formed a steeple with his hands and placed it under his chin. "Lily, I've considered this at length. As a father, I want my sons to find good women. I may not be the best matchmaker in the business, but I know good stock when I see it. You and your sisters are good stock, and I'd love to have you in this family."

When she hesitated, Horton added, "Please think it over and let me know."

Lily thought it over that night and accepted the following morning. She had planned to get married —albeit to a gentleman of fine upbringing—but she admitted a sense of excitement at the thought of joining her life to Jasper's. She knew she wasn't indifferent to his hooded glances and quick smiles.

After her decision, she did her best to catch Jasper's eye, but the more she tried, the more she failed. He ignored her feeble attempts and refused to engage in conversation. As the silent treatment continued, he had lapsed into deep-ridged frowns at the mere sight of her tender smile.

After countless tries, Lily came up with another plan. She discussed it with his mother, Running

Deer, who suggested that the two venture out for an afternoon outing. Jasper loved them, so Lily agreed with the idea and made plans to take Jasper to dinner, which would hopefully splash some cheer on his dour face.

Jasper crept downstairs and cast a wary eye around the premises. A quiet atmosphere invaded the lower floor, and he expelled a deep sigh. Peace and contentment. It felt good.

His stomach gurgled and reminded him of the lateness of the hour. *Time for a morsel to eat.* He rushed to the kitchen, but a shadow crossed his path and stopped him in his tracks. He hadn't moved fast enough. *Lily.*

"Did you plan to avoid me forever?"

The hurt tone showed his subterfuge, and Jasper groaned. He should have scouted the terrain better. "I'm sorry, I didn't see you there."

A glimmer of hurt flashed in her eyes. "Is that why you've been hiding?"

Jasper relented and felt like a heel. He didn't want to hurt her. She had such a fragile personality, and burst into tears at the least provocation.

At the sight of her bright eyes, he hurried to stave off the waterworks. "No, I planned to catch up on my studies. Thought I might join my father in his orange business."

The waterworks evaporated, and joy spread across her face. Jasper bit his tongue and chided himself. The lie had slipped out without him realizing what he meant to say.

"That is wonderful news! I know he will be happy to have you join him." She smiled and continued, "I have news of my own, Jasper: I wish to take you out for dinner tonight. There's a lovely little place in town called Mabelle's with lots of ferns and nice windows. Will you come with me?"

Jasper hoped he didn't appear as shocked as he felt. "You want to take me to dinner?"

She blinked at the incredulous tone and her shoulders drooped. Tears clung to her lashes, and she mumbled, "I'm so sorry if I offended you by asking."

Jasper tilted his head and did his best to hide a brief smile. Her constant wailing could put the rain to shame. "No, you didn't offend me."

When her gaze turned hopeful, he stepped closer and lowered his head, "I'll go with you, and Mabelle's is a great choice—I love her food. She's known me since I was a boy; put me over her legs to swat my behind more times than I can count."

Her giggles tugged her lips upward, and soon they both laughed over the thought.

"That must have been a sight. She must be a special person for your father to allow such a thing."

Jasper grinned, his thoughts going back in time. "Oh yes. I think my Pa wanted to marry her, but my Ma got in the way once she came into the picture. One look at her and my Pa lost his mind—and his heart. He said the winter snow turned her hair into beautiful ebony waves when she rode across the molten plains to meet him."

Lily sighed. "That sounds so nice. Do you write poetry?"

Jasper stepped back in stupefied disbelief. The woman must be daft. "Me? I couldn't do that to save my life."

She didn't agree with his negative assessment, and her eyes sparkled. "I think you could write the most wonderful poetry, if you tried."

"I don't know about that, Lily. But I will go to Mabelle's—"

"Let's have a picnic sometime, too. Your father tells me the Santa Ana River is nice this time of year. We can prepare a basket."

Jasper blinked in bemusement and tried not to be embarrassed. Two offers in one day? It had to be a record. "Sounds good."

"Excellent." She scampered away with a quick reminder over her shoulder: "Don't forget to write a few lines of poetry. Can't wait to read it!"

He mumbled an inane reply and continued to the kitchen. *Poetry? Me? What an idea!* When his heart pounded with an unnatural rhythm, Jasper groaned. He didn't understand why Lily affected him on such a level.

CHAPTER 9

Mabelle's inn offered a thrilling outing for Lily. With a wide grin, she allowed Jasper to lead her into the dining room with its lavish mahogany furnishings, crafted wall coverings, and tasteful lamps.

Elegant drapery framed the windows and bright potted plants graced the corners. The chatter of the patrons lent a cheerful air, and the curling scents tickled Lily's nose. Her stomach rumbled, and she giggled. She couldn't wait to indulge in a tasty dinner.

When they sat at a corner table draped in a rose print tablecloth with a view to the boardwalk, Lily arranged her dress. She wanted to be as comfortable as possible and enjoy the time spent with Jasper.

A furtive glance showed the admiration smoldering in his gaze, and she felt pleased to know her efforts had been successful. Her pale shoulders rose in a nice contrast to the navy-blue gown with a rounded neckline and V waist. The snow-white ribbons and lace that adorned the neck and edges added a delicate touch. Stray tendrils fell from the clever up-sweep intertwined with bright blue flowers, and her smile enhanced her glow.

When the maître d' arrived with a menu, he flashed a smile brighter than the sun. He tipped an invisible hat and said, "Welcome to Mabelle's, Mr. Wallace. Nice to see you here again, sir, and the lady…?"

Jasper introduced Lily with a lazy grin. "Miss Lily Barrington from the east. She's visiting us until my sister-in-law comes to fetch her."

The smile got broader. "That is wonderful news. Here's the menu. I'll bring a glass of water to get started, and please take your time."

When he left them to choose their meal, Lily reached for her glass of water and took a deep gulp. She turned to Jasper and fanned in vigorous strokes to relieve the heat stinging her cheeks. "Do you recommend any meals in particular?"

Before could respond, the sound of a raised voice

interrupted their pleasant evening. "Well now, what a surprise. Fancy meeting you here tonight."

Lily gawked at the vision in fine gossamer silk and exotic jewelry. The newcomer gushed over Jasper with overbearing familiarity. Lily watched the back-and-forth and felt like a third wheel in a big loop.

When Jasper made the introductions, the woman's gaze hardened. She flashed an insincere smile and held out a gloved hand.

"So, you're Lily. How sweet. As Jasper said, my name is Daisy May Meriwether. I belong to the Meriwethers of Riverside, a well-esteemed family around these parts."

The proud voice dripped in glacial tones and offered no friendly quarter. Lily turned to Jasper. She felt intimidated and didn't understand the virulent dislike coming from Daisy May.

A frown clouded Jasper's eyes and a pulse beat at the edge of his lips. "Lily, Daisy May is a neighbor and friend."

Daisy bristled at the term 'friend' and her mouth tilted in a sneer. "I don't think *friend* is what you would call it, Jasper. Shall I tell your darling how many times you've been at my door and at what hours you've arrived?"

Lily gasped at the indecent nature of the question. Had the woman lost her senses? She seemed confident enough. Perhaps she had cause to speak in such a manner. Lily guessed Daisy must have a strong relationship with Jasper to try such unladylike behavior.

Lily closed her eyes for a moment. Tears stung her lids, and she took a shuddering breath. Her appetite vanished, leaving her weak and spent.

Unable to bear the disruptive presence, she stood on trembling legs and turned to Daisy. Her voice sounded odd even in her ears. "It was nice to meet you. Jasper, can you take me home, please?"

Daisy May jumped to her feet, her eyes alive in fury. "Please don't leave on my account. I'd like to tickle your ear with Jasper's exploits around town."

Lily stepped back in shock. She had no intentions of dealing with a viper in disguise. "Jasper, can we please leave?"

Daisy gritted her teeth and said, "Shall I walk you both home, Jasper dear? I've done it many times before."

The edges of Jasper's mouth formed a thin line. His voice bore a thread of steel, and he commanded, "Stop this at once, Daisy May. You have done enough damage for one evening. Go home and find something to do."

Daisy May wilted at Jasper's unbreakable tone. Her shoulders sagged, and she cast anxious eyes over his hard face. When he offered his elbow to Lily, she murmured, "I see. Please excuse me for interrupting your evening."

Daisy stumbled over to a corner table, and sat in the shadows. Jasper ignored her and walked over to the maître d' to apologize. When they left the inn, Lily's tears trickled over flushed cheeks. How could such a lovely evening end in such disastrous results?

CHAPTER 10

JASPER ROSE WITH THE SUN. IT WAS JUST PAST FIVE, and he had important things to do. Lily had mentioned a picnic the day before, and he planned to get everything ready ahead of time. At the break of dawn, he hurried to the kitchen and woke the housekeeper; he urged her to prepare a meal fit for a princess.

In between shaving and choosing comfortable clothing, Daisy May came to mind. Jasper cringed. He had to visit her and lay bare his guilt. He had to tell her how sorry he was for his actions. Over the years, he had grown comfortable with Daisy's insults. How foolish he had been!

His ear picked up the bustle of morning life and

the muffled talk of his parents on the landing. *Time to go.*

After breakfast, Jasper drover Lily to a sloping bluff near the river. The noise of the town faded, replaced by the quiet sounds of gurgles under a cloudless sky. He loved the surroundings and often rode out to find peace and to lay his troubled thoughts to rest.

Jasper spread a gingham blanket on the soft earth and arranged the basket and dishes. Lily watched him with a cheerful smile and offered to help. "Can't let you do it by yourself."

Jasper grinned, pleased with her actions. He turned to the inland mountains, and the billowed clouds over the horizon. "This land is a land of promise. Did you know that?"

When she shook her head, he promised to tell her Riverside's history. "Before we get started on a long story, can you wash this plate for me? It fell out on the way."

Lily's face softened to a tender glow, and she skipped to the riverbank. "I'll be happy to help you. Be right back."

Jasper glanced at the sky and thanked the good Lord for allowing Lily to enter his life. What had she said when he drove her from the station? *With faith, all things are possible?* How could he miss such wise words over the years?

His admitted his wastrel nature had led him adrift, and he cringed at the wasted years. Thoughts of Daisy May surfaced again. He should've treated her better than he had. The fact was, he should've been more care—

"Jasper!"

Lily's urgent cry struck fear in Jasper's heart, and he rushed to her side. When he came to a shuddering halt, his gaze clung to her pale face and trembling lips. "What is it? Are you ill?"

She stumbled into his arms and collapsed against his chest, her breathing labored. Jasper held her in a tight embrace, wondering what had happened. When she raised her right hand, his heart stopped.

Two bruised puncture wounds with crimson globs stained her blue-veined skin. The sound of a slither in the grass caught his ear, and he spun with Lily in his arms. He spied the shimmering scales of a snake scampering into the grass, and sucked in a deep breath. His mind told him what his heart knew to be true. *My God! It's poisonous.*

Jasper's mind exploded in unspeakable fear. The poison had to be drained; if it wasn't, she'd never make it back to town. He rushed to apply pressure to stop the venom from reaching her heart.

When she slumped over in a dead faint, he laid her on the ground. He kept the right arm low and used a sharp blade to drain as much of the poison as he could.

He kept an eye on her progress and spied a bright red flush creeping over her skin. Her chest rose in rapid succession and the beat of her pulse thundered beneath his fingertips.

With fervent pleas and prayerful utterances, Jasper gathered Lily into his arms. He eyed the molten orb of the noon sun and calculated the time. *Dear God. Please don't let me be too late.*

CHAPTER 11

ONE WEEK LATER

"Lily, dearest, open your eyes."

Lily groaned, her world a haze of semi-conscious thoughts. Random images danced across her eyes fused to her lids. Her limbs hung in aimless lines and reminded her of wooden puppets without strings.

"Please, dearest. Open your eyes. It's me, Willow."

Lily frowned, her brow rumpling. She stirred and her voice cracked in raspy tones. "Willow? She's not here. She's in California married to a frontiersman and the kids are sick. With fever."

Gentle laughter flowed at her matter-of-fact statement. "Yes, that's right, but my boys are fine now. I'm here and I want you to open your eyes."

Lily's eyelids rose, and she focused her nebulous gaze. The drawn curtains allowed sunlight to fill the surroundings with cheerful warmth. An embroidered pink coverlet lay across the bed in a room decorated with peaches and cream, and bright paintings adorned the walls.

Willow sat next to the bed and Lily reached out with a smile. "Dearest sister, it's you!"

Willow buried Lily in a firm embrace, and her tear-filled eyes overflowed with joy. "You had us so worried. We thought you would not make it, but Running Deer promised to make you well. She has nursed you day and night for the past week. I am so grateful for her help."

In the darkest throes of the nightmare, Lily recalled a soothing voice and gentle hands. "Sorry for the trouble I caused. I didn't see the creature until it was too late. I think I called for Jasper, but I can't… I can't remember…"

Willow's eyes met hers with a teasing grin. "He's been at your side, pestering the doctor to tears. He refused to give up hope even after your mother told him things looked grim. I don't think he's ever prayed before, but he never left your side or ceased to beg for your life. I'll tell him you're awake."

When Willow strolled to the open door, Lily cried out, "No, please wait."

At Willow's frown, Lily fingered her wrinkled dress and dull, matted waves. She could just imagine how frightful she looked. "I don't mean to be vain, but would you please help me get dressed and comb my hair?"

Willow flashed a relieved grin. "Modesty and propriety above all things. Never let it be said that the Barrington women are slovenly or ill attired."

Lily nodded, thankful for her sister's understanding. She'd made it against the odds. It was a miracle, and she didn't intend to take it for granted. Grateful for a second chance, she whispered, "*Jasper, I can't wait to tell you how much I love you.*"

CHAPTER 12

JASPER CHUCKLED AND EXAMINED HIS COLLAR IN THE full-length mirror. *Too tight.* He had to get the tailor to remove the extra button. He glanced at the wall clock: twenty-four hours left. In one day, he and Lily would satisfy his father's wishes as they agreed to become man and wife. Anticipation shot though him at the thought and he wallowed in a contented daze.

"Looking good, son."

The sound of his father's voice brought a smile to Jasper's face. "Thanks, Pa. Just need to get this button removed. Is Lily alright?"

Horton stepped forward and patted him on the shoulder. "She's fine. Your mother is getting her ready for tomorrow's event, and she looks as bonny as a bright new fiddle."

Jasper grinned. He thought of their future together and prayed for a blessing. "Pa, I've been meaning to talk to you about the plantation. I can help watch those trees for you—that is, if you still want me on your team."

Horton's eyes glowed with pride. "Jasper, you're my son; of course I'd love for you to carry on in the family business. Nothing would make me more proud." He wiped a stray tear from his eye, clearly moved by Jasper's intentions. Straightening up, he cleared his throat and continued, "Enough said about that, now. As for this wife of yours, I trust you will treat her with silk gloves. She's got a heart a mile wide and ten oceans deep. Don't be riling her too much and keep her safe. Got that?"

Jasper saluted with a cheeky smile. "Yes, sir."

Horton ruffled his hair and stepped back with a pensive gaze. "I'm guessing you need to take care of other personal matters today? Am I right?"

Jasper nodded and expelled a deep sigh. "Yes, I have to visit Daisy May. Tell Lily not to eat lunch without me."

When his father left, Jasper's thoughts turned to the task at hand. No better time than the present.

CHAPTER 13

Daisy May swallowed hard as her world toppled on its head. When Jasper appeared unannounced, her heart had drummed a joyous beat.

Before he could speak, she ushered him into the tea room and ordered refreshments. She kept up a cheerful chatter until he said the words that ripped a void in her heart.

"Daisy, I'm sorry, but I have to tell you… there can be nothing between us. Lily is the girl for me."

Daisy's blood roared through her ears. She struggled for a foothold on her emotions but fell flat. "You're marrying *Lily?* Why? I thought *we* would marry and form a home together!"

Jasper nodded, his eyes shadowed. "Daisy, can you please forgive me? I never meant to hurt you.

And I can see my foolish behavior has caused you pain."

Daisy held her breath. Pain? He didn't understand what it meant. She arched her chin and held her head high. Other women may cry and plead, but not her. She was a Meriwether, and they weathered life's storms with pride and dignity. "What is there to forgive? I am a fool, and Lily has won the race. My horse was too slow and stumbled in the final turn."

Jasper shook his head. "I've treated you as the sister I never had, but I should have made my intentions straight from the beginning. Daisy, I want to be your friend—that is, if you will let me."

Tears burned Daisy's lids, but she held them back. She reached into her silk purse and removed a peacock fan, then cooled herself with vigorous strokes and turned away. "I will have to speak with you later. Please leave."

When Jasper walked toward the door, Daisy struggled to get her final words past her lips. "I... I hope you and Lily find happiness."

Jasper paused, his hand on the door handle. "I understand, Daisy. I wish you the best in your life."

Daisy watched her dreams crumble in dust at his departure, and wondered if she'd ever know joy again.

CHAPTER 14

Jasper and Lily sat side by side on the porch swing watching the sunset. Vibrant multicolored hues lit up the evening sky encircling the promise of a new day.

Lily wondered how her life had changed in such a short time, but she did not question the blessing. Still, she had to ask one question. "Jasper, are you sure Daisy May isn't the woman for you?"

At his odd glance, she rushed to explain, "I'd never try to destroy your happiness. I want you to know that… that I love you enough to let you go."

Jasper's face drained of color. He stared at her in shock and whispered, "You *love* me, Lily?"

Lily bowed her head, her response muffled by her lowered chin. "Yes, Jasper, I do. I think it started that day at the station. And now, it's settled in my heart."

Jasper whistled and shook his head. "I never would've guessed. I know you chased me around, but I must admit to being blinded by a good hunk of hardheadedness."

Lily smiled though tears. "I love everything about you, Jasper—even your good hunk of hard-headedness."

He laughed in relief. "Well, that sounds mighty fine. Let me tell you what you mean to me."

When he fished out a piece of paper from the inside of his jacket, Lily frowned until he began to read in his deep, husky voice: "Dearest Lily, when I see your eyes, I drown in the ocean of your gaze. And when I see your hair, it reminds me of the sunlight that gilds the land. And by the beat of your heart, I can find my way home."

At her bemusement, he flashed a self-conscious grin. "I know it's not poetry, but it comes from inside my heart."

When she kept silent, he gave her an uncertain look. "It's the best I can do."

Lily caught her breath in wonder and raised her hand to his cheek. Her voice echoed as soft as her touch. "Jasper, it's beautiful because it's from you. As long as it comes from your heart, it means the world to me."

He cupped her face, his gaze tender and soft. "Lily... I love you, too." He placed an arm around shoulders and drew her close, "I really do."

Lily leaned into his embrace, her mind a web of gentle bliss. She had found her own happily ever after, and she couldn't wait to see what joys their life together would bring.

THE END

MAIL ORDER BRIDE ROSE

BRIDES OF RIVERSIDE

CHAPTER 1

RIVERSIDE, CALIFORNIA. APRIL, 1897.

GET MARRIED TO A STRANGER FROM THE EAST... WHEN pigs fly across the desert.

Joseph Wallace shot his father a heated glance and clenched his chiseled jaw. Beads of sweat peppered his brow and his heart hammered.

He remembered his childhood, huddling behind his favorite gnarled oak. Its majestic branches had offered an escape from his troubled thoughts, and he wanted its protection again.

"Pa, marriage is not for me."

Horton Wallace, patriarch of the Wallace clan, twirled the fine hairs of his frosted mustache. His tailored black suit and gleaming Stetson with silver trim showed the epitome of Western grandeur. A youthful look twinkled in his moss green eyes, and the faint lines on this brow belied his sixty years. He brushed aside Joseph's halfhearted refusal with a boisterous laugh. "Nonsense, my boy. Marriage will do you good. I can attest to that. Your ma has given me happiness for years."

Joseph licked his dry lips. The three-piece suit with matching waistcoat and dark trousers enhanced his muscular frame and hewn shoulders. Compelling teal eyes complemented dark, clipped hair that fell in handsome waves around his ears.

His brain swirled with a thousand thoughts, but no good excuse came to mind. The silken red tie around his throat choked the flow of air and he tugged it loose. He signaled the clean-shaven, solemn servant and ordered refreshments to stall for time.

"Pa, why don't we have a cup of coffee? Got your favorite brew from Jim's mercantile. Heard they plan to expand into the next county."

Horton shrugged, unconcerned with the news or the offer of something hot to drink. "No time for that now, my boy. Let's talk about your marriage. I know this woman will make your home complete."

Joseph groaned and lowered his head. *Great. Just great.* Behind his forbearer's devil-may-care facade churned a calculating mind—a mind focused on him. He'd prefer a rattlesnake for dinner or the hide of the toughest buffalo for supper. To change the discussion, he pointed to the strewn papers across his gleaming desk.

"Pa, I can't do this now. I'm running late on my business and need to get things done."

The plans to inaugurate Joseph's restaurant—The Golden River—lay in a vast array of snow-white sheets with scribbled notes. His plan to tap into the constant gold fever resonated with his peers and parents alike. Everyone championed his intentions to serve the miners more than charred pork, salted ham, and hard biscuits.

Joseph prided himself on a meticulous menu based on the delicacies of the finest European cuisine. He wanted his clients to enjoy nothing but the best culinary delights with a whiff of the East and great helpings of the West. With the opening a month away, he needed to devote his time to get the final details in place. An offer of marriage could ruin that plan.

He raised his head and collided with his father's expectant gaze; so much for that thought.

"Pa, I know this means a great deal to you to set us boys up with good wives. Joshua and Jasper are doing good, I hear."

Horton grinned from ear to ear, and Joseph sighed. He knew his father took his job as family head more serious than most, and he respected his position. As one of the most upstanding and successful families in the neighborhood, the Wallaces set the standard many followed.

Riverside had no saloons that disturbed the peace and a tranquil life pervaded the town. Joseph liked it that way. He had heard enough stories of shanty-towns overrun with brawling saloons, lawlessness and large-scale shootouts. He could never set up a restaurant in such tawdry conditions.

"Rose is here, Joseph. Got in yesterday morning on the Southern Pacific. Met her a short time ago, and let me tell you...she's a special girl. I know she's good for you."

Yes, so you've said for the past hour. When the servant brought two steaming cups of coffee with salted biscuits, Joseph took a hasty sip and scalded his tongue.

"Jumping Jehoshaphat!"

Horton doubled over in laughter. "Drink slower,

boy, and taste before drinking. Haven't I taught you that?"

Yes, and how to get your own way. Joseph set the steaming mug back on the table. He hated it when his father used coercion, and wondered if he might use the same tactics when he became a father. The unbidden thought shot lightning bolts through him and he squirmed. *What am I thinking?*

He dragged his mind back to the present and groaned, "Pa, don't I have better things to do than get hitched?"

Horton's easygoing expression vanished. He crossed his arms and said, "Bah! If I leave *you* to decide, you won't do a thing. That's why. A solid union will help you better organize your life. I happen to think Rose is a good woman, and she needs a good man. Forgot to mention, I want a few grandkids, too. Six or seven will do mighty fine."

Joseph choked on his second sip of coffee and spewed warm droplets all over the table. He fished a handkerchief from the inside of his coat and wiped the dark stains in furious strokes. *Six or seven children?* Never.

Besides, he didn't subscribe to the idea of marital bliss. Women had a way of interfering with his dreams, and he didn't want to start a new relationship—with the last disastrous one fresh in his mind. "To find a good woman is impossible. They have nothing on their mind other than new clothes, moonlit rides, and shining rings on trigger-happy fingers."

"Never heard such nonsense in my life." Horton said and watched his son struggle to compose himself. "Your mother is a good woman. Have you forgotten that?"

Joseph's swift rush of anger melted into warm memories. His mother's tender glance, smiling eyes, and soft expression filled his mind. Running Deer had been the only reason he tolerated womankind. Her constant love and devotion over the years had been a shining light. Most women couldn't hold a candle to her. In his experience, they left much to be desired. "My mother is a saint on earth, but she's the only one I know."

Horton sniffed and his eyes narrowed. "Your brothers will disagree on that point. They've found excellent wives, and the Barrington women are fine stock. Just come off your high horse and you'll see for yourself."

Yeah, and when I'm in doubt, my horse will do the thinking. Spent at the verbiage, Joseph rushed to end the conversation in diplomatic tones. "Yes, Father. I know you're right. Can we talk on this later? I need to get back to work. I want the inauguration to be perfect."

Horton accepted the not-so-subtle hint and rose. He adjusted his Stetson over his frosted grey hair and rocked back on his heels. "Come to the house for dinner tonight."

When Joseph opened his mouth to decline, his father sweetened the offer: "Your mother is having everyone over and wants you there. You don't have to polish your righteous principles. Just eat your dinner. Deal?"

Joseph agreed, thoughts of his mother in mind. If she requested his presence, he had to go. "Sure. I'll come."

After Horton's departure, Joseph rested his head in his hands. He didn't want another frazzled female nipping at his heels, but he might have to do the honors required of him.

Disgusted at the turn of events, he strolled across the pinewood floor and gazed beyond the wavy glass window. The opening led beyond the wrap around porch to a wide expanse of cerulean skies and cumulus clouds hovering over the town.

A soaring eagle rose on effortless wings, and

Joseph longed to do the same. A new relationship filled him with dread and soured his tongue. He wondered if Rose might abandon him at the altar with his heart in his hand, or leave him to face the barren days and empty nights—alone.

CHAPTER 2

Rose Barrington wandered along the sunlit path and watched the birds flutter among the verdant trees that lined the driveway. The two-floor Victorian house stood in graceful splendor, and she admired the distinctive clapboard trim, curving porch, and stained glass windows. Even the oval ceiling, crisscrossed beams, decorative light fixtures, and gleaming hardwood floors enchanted her and reminded her of home.

Along the drive, she inspected the low-lying fence and the well-swept path, flanked by giant trees with bright green leaves and plenty of shade. A cool spring breeze stirred the tendrils of her blonde hair, and she raised both hands to embrace the light. It felt good to be alive.

Her gaze rose beyond the path and focused on the road leading to town. She loved the meandering roads and rambling valleys that spread across the scenic landscape. In place of a monotonous, arid climate, the county basked in colorful seasons interspersed with verdant trees, copper sand, bare slopes, and floral blooms.

It had taken over a week to make the trip from Maine to California after she'd received the summons from Horton Wallace. He'd asked her to marry his son Joseph, and Rose had agreed after the success of her two sisters. Willow and Lily had found excellent husbands, and Rose hoped to do the same. She had yet to meet Joseph, but she imagined him to be a noble gentleman with a heart of gold.

At her arrival, she learned that her sisters had left for San Bernardino with their husbands. Horton told her they'd return in one month, and offered her a place to stay in the meantime. Rose accepted, touched at his kindness and the opportunity to know Joseph better.

The sound of turning wheels interrupted her musings and diverted her thoughts. She watched a one-horse buggy amble down the road and come to a full stop at the edge of the drive. A tall, well-dressed stranger stepped out at the edge of the road and adjusted his suit. Satisfied, he turned and made his way toward her.

At a distance, he exuded confidence and vitality in each measured step. When he caught sight of Rose's curious gaze, he drew to a halt. His penetrating glance stripped her from head to toe, and she blinked in surprise. A thunderous frown marred his perfect brow, and she wondered why he had such a dour look on his handsome face.

When he stepped to the side to continue his walk, Rose whispered a breathless greeting. Despite his ill-mannered behavior, she did not want to treat him in kind. The Good Book said to treat others as you want to be treated, and she did her best to follow the Golden Rule. "Good morning...uh...sir?"

"Are you Rose Barrington—my *supposed* future bride?"

Joseph Wallace? Was it really him? Rose balked at the accusing tone and stepped back. The guttural question revealed an unpleasant undercurrent she didn't understand. Still, her treacherous heart skipped a beat.

Her eyes clung to his well-dressed appearance, and she wagered he'd outshine the most refined gentlemen. Rose felt like a wallflower in comparison, and concluded her plain dress with faded flowers and patched elbows did nothing to enhance her feminine attributes.

The heat rose in her cheeks and she croaked, "Yes, my name is Rose Ba—Barrington."

He nodded as though aware of the answer she'd give. "You are not what I expected."

You mean plain and drab? Rose bit her tongue, surprised she hadn't spoken the words outright. She knew her summer-blue eyes—fringed with gold-tipped lashes—drowned her face and gave her an owlish look. Her lips had none of the plumpness she desired and lay in two thin strips between high cheeks. They might have enhanced her appearance, but were too blunt to soften the lines of her face. Rose's one saving grace lay in her thick mane of shiny blonde hair, which she had smoothed and twisted into a golden bun atop her head.

"I'm sorry to disappoint you."

He raised his brow at her matter-of-fact response. "Why should it matter if you disappoint me?"

Because I hoped to be your bride? Rose chided herself for the intense feelings of insecurity. She knew it did not matter what lay on the outside—what was inside a person made the difference. When she stayed silent, he murmured, "I'm curious, Rose. What did you hope to discover in Riverside?"

Good question. Rose scrambled for a neutral response. In her life, she strove to be level-headed and centered. Even her sisters championed her amiable spirit. If anyone could create calm and poise, it was Rose. If anyone could soothe the ugly nature of a beast, it was Rose. If anyone could temper the booming thunder, it was Rose.

But her unique skills flew out to pasture at the compelling glance in Joseph's gaze, and left her disconcerted. *So much for being level-headed.*

"Well, um—I hoped to start a different life, and I hoped to become a part of yours." Rose cringed at her comment and hoped it didn't sound childish and naïve.

Joseph shrugged, unimpressed with her breathless statement. He glanced at the papers in his hands and said, "Right. Listen here. My father believes we should wed. I do not understand why he thinks this way, but you must get him to change his mind."

Get him to change his mind?

Rose hoped she hadn't heard right. He wanted to

break the engagement? Dark clouds gathered overhead and the warm air cooled. A sudden, sharp wind tore at the hem of her dress and a litter of leaves frolicked in the breeze. Thunder rumbled in the distance and damp air tickled her nose.

Rose hovered in a daze, her thoughts as dark as the approaching storm. "I'm sorry. I don't understand what you mean."

He eyed the encroaching darkness and frowned. With a sharp breath, he said, "I've tried the marriage thing. Got myself a nice lady and chased her from here to Tombstone like a lovesick fool. She spurned me for months until she said yes. Made plans for the wedding in a jiffy and got myself spruced like a dandy, then ran her to the altar on a nice spring day. Do you know where the lady was?"

Not there, I'd wager. Rose lacked a suitable response in reply to the bitter slant of his lips. Instead, she gripped the folds of her dress and hoped her face didn't appear as drawn as she felt.

Joseph smiled at her reticence, but the tilt of his lips did not thaw the frost in his eyes. "She ran off with my best friend from childhood. Left me a note to tell me how sorry she was and said something about her hopes for me to find true love. Got that?"

Rose didn't. A gust of wind pelted them with

drizzled pellets and they rushed toward the house. They reached the porch when the downpour began.

Rose watched the slanted sheets of rain drench the ground, and allowed the steady sound to soothe her. She wondered if Joseph realized how scarred he'd become from the event in his life and how it affected his outlook. Maybe he needed her more than he thought. "I am sorry to hear of your pain. It must be a difficult experience."

His fists curled around the notes in his hands, and he rejected her sympathy with rigid shoulders. "I am not hurt—just tired. Besides, I have bigger things to do. I plan to open a restaurant in one month. I'm serving miners and their families who prefer a more elegant meal than a simple bite of mutton to eat. This is my concern—*not* marriage."

The firm note in his voice dented Rose's heart. She turned away from his iron-clad expression and tried to think on positive things. In the deep recesses of her mind, she'd planned to become a school-teacher someday. Children filled her with joy, and she knew their agile minds needed a firm but loving hand. It might be a great idea, since Joseph didn't want—

"Do you know about fixing up a place right and

proper? You know, napkins, the proper fork, knife, glass, and all that?"

Rose started, surprised Joseph had spoken to her in such a curious way. She eyed him suspiciously, careful to keep her response unaffected. "Yes, I do. My parents entertained often in the past, and I planned the evening dinners."

He raised a brow at her confident statement and considered her response. Then he waved her over to the porch swing and waited for her to sit.

"I think you can help me to do something."

Do what? Run behind your buggy for sport? Ashamed at her mean-spirited thought, Rose lowered her gaze and prayed for forgiveness. It must be hard for Joseph to trust a woman, and she needed to remember that. "How can I help you?"

"I want to offer my customers a sample of my culinary arts. I hope that when they spread out around the country, they will take the news to others. Word of mouth is one of the best ways to let others know what we offer."

Rose agreed, but wondered what he wanted from her. "And how can I help you make *your* dreams come true?"

Joseph blinked at the undercurrent in her voice, but refrained from mentioning it. "If you'd help me to get my place ready, I'd appreciate it. Then we can tell everyone we didn't make it, and leave it at that."

Rose squared her shoulders and raised her chin. Why not? She had no immediate plans and getting her school-teaching idea off the ground would take time. "Yes, I can help you get your restaurant ready. After it's done, I will tell your father it did not work out between us and I'll go. Will that please you?"

Joseph flashed an admiring glance at the resolute tilt of her chin. "Yes, if you're willing. The truth is the restaurant can use a woman's gentle touch. I can give you an excellent reference when it's over that will open doors in any county around these parts. Oh, and one more thing."

At her expectant gaze, he said, "Don't tell my father or anyone else. This is between you and me. That will keep them off my saddles including well-wishers, and give me the time I need."

Deception and untruths? Rose thought hard. She felt unsettled at his request, but if she didn't share the news with anyone, was it really be a deception? Could it be an untruth if she refused to elaborate on their arrangements?

Her lips would not utter an outright lie, but she didn't have to share intimate details either. The plan might work and then she'd leave at the end of the month with her self-respect intact.

When she raised troubled eyes to Joseph's cool glance, Rose hoped she looked poised and in control. "Yes, I will keep this between us. No one else will know—not even my sisters."

"Excellent. That is the best news I've heard today. I know I can count on you to help me get things up and running. You seem like a capable woman. Then you can go on your own way when you're done. No sense in muddying up the waterhole by sticking around. Deal?"

Rose caught her breath. She marveled at how her future intended wielded compliments and insults with the superb skill of a matador. He needed to learn how to treat others with more kindness.

A sudden thought came to her, and she held her breath. What if she could get him to change his mind and *want* her to stay? One month might be enough to burrow into his heart and make him see how much he needed her. It would take patience, kindness, and a loving heart, but it might work. After all… *love bears all things, believes all things, hopes all things, endures all things.*

Once the idea took hold, it refused to go away. Rose averted her face to hide the gleam in her eyes.

She didn't want Joseph to get suspicious and change his tune. But a niggling sensation of excitement brewed in the back of her mind. She extended her right hand to seal the pact.

"Yes, it's a deal."

When he engulfed her hand in his own, she whispered a prayer in her heart. *All things are possible if you have faith.*

CHAPTER 3

THE NEXT MORNING, ROSE STAYED IN BED MUCH longer than she intended. Not even the sweet sounds of the early morning birds induced her to start the day. Her gaze wandered to the corner of the ceiling, where a mottled spider wove an intricate web. The little creature worked tirelessly to engineer the crystal threads in the right shape and size before resting. Rose admired the hard labor and wondered why she couldn't rest the previous night.

She admitted the evening had been fraught with unwelcomed emotions and concern. Thoughts of dinner—an elaborate feast—and Joseph's tight face crowded her thoughts. Despite his earlier plea for help and her harebrained scheme to make him fall in love, he'd done his best to dismiss her presence—

until the inevitable happened. Rose closed her eyes and relived the instant she wanted to disappear under the cracks in the floor.

After the brisk drops of rain had fallen to a gentle patter, the sun burst forth in a blaze of glory. The grey, stormy skies melted into a cerulean blanket and a tincture of freshness lingered in the air.

Rose had enjoyed the cool evening and spent the rest of the day exploring the perfumed gardens chock-full of milk maids, orchids and evergreen shrubs with camellia-like flowers in scented white, pink, and yellow blooms. Rich lavender-purple lilacs added a touch of exotic flair, and stone circled ponds overflowed with water lilies.

The hours spent led to a relaxed temperament, and Rose later prepared for the night with little else on her mind than the sweet scent of flowers.

That evening, dinner turned into a lavish affair in honor of her arrival. The gold-papered walls shimmered, and polished cutlery adorned the oak table with rough edges. Large windows—left ajar—let in the starlit night air, and a gleaming fixture with three lamps dangled from the ornate ceiling.

A brocade table runner with embroidered blooms lay under two tall golden candelabra with scented candles. Floral napkins complemented the well-laid table and matched the runner in the center. Rose loved the elegant fixtures and delighted in the tasty meal.

Among the tall crystal glasses and gay laughter, Joseph ignored her fumbling attempts to talk to him. When she tried to engage him in conversation, he muttered one-syllable comments and turned to the other guests. His actions shut her out, and Rose retreated to her plate. She hoped her despair didn't show, and did her best to smile from time to time.

Horton Wallace—seated at the head of the table—caught her furtive glances and strained expression. "Rose, my dear. Why so downhearted? This is *your* evening. Celebrate and be cheerful. Eat more food and put meat on your bones."

When the guests turned to her with degrees of curiosity, Rose managed a halfhearted smile and popped a sweetened slice of carrot in her mouth. It tumbled around for an eternity before she swallowed. The mound of mashed potatoes with tender swirls of gravy came next. Much more palatable and easier to digest. She tried the grilled and juicy tenderloin steak when Horton's voice boomed again: "Have you set a date for the wedding? Share it with us so we can get ready. Got to roast a pig and kill a cow."

Rose froze with a startled face, and her heart stopped. She tried to think of a glib excuse, but drew a blank. Her eyes locked on Joseph with an unspoken plea. Unruffled and at ease, he raised his glass with a wide grin. "Now, Pa, don't spoil the surprise. You will find out in due time. Let's enjoy our meal and discuss my wedding plans another day."

The guests had offered bouts of praise and congratulations, much to Rose's chagrin. In keeping with the plan, she smiled and accepted their gracious words, but within her heart, she felt like a fraud. The sensation grew and still hadn't died by morning.

Rose dismissed her memories and turned to the rays of the sun streaming through the gossamer curtains. Cheerful warmth filled the room decorated in peaches and cream with white-painted furnishings. Beyond the windows, a bright morning blossomed with endless possibilities. No sense in staying in bed.

She hurried to wash up before breakfast and chose a simple frock to wear. She wondered what new ideas Joseph had in mind, but vowed to do her best to help him succeed. He had promised to come in the morning for an early start.

With one eye on the clock, she finished styling

her hair. Nothing more than a simple bun twisted at the nape, and a dab or two of rose water. When a bleak expression stared back from the gilded mirror, Rose arranged her face with a pleasant smile. She didn't intend to mope around for one month and make her life miserable.

Her feet skimmed the polished floor as she raced downstairs to the breakfast room. A steaming pot of tea, a plate of fresh biscuits and a bowl of scrambled eggs stood waiting. After thanking the cook for her kindness and generosity, Rose ate her breakfast in amiable silence.

She had just finished her second cup of tea when Joseph strolled in with a frown. "Still eating? We need to get a move on. Strike while the iron is hot, you know?"

Rose tried to stay calm over the pitter-patter in her heart. She groped for something witty to say, but the thoughts fizzled and died under the onslaught of Joseph's scented soap. As usual, his attire fell in impeccable lines. She should have taken more time with her clothing.

"There's no need to glare, Miss Barrington. I was just making idle conversation, nothing more."

Rose started, unaware of the glower on her face. She had no reason to get upset with him, and felt ashamed to have displayed such negative emotions. "Forgive me. I didn't mean to glare."

He stepped forward and consulted his pocket watch. "Shall we go now? I cannot waste the day on your dawdling."

Rose gasped at this coarse command; this was not how she wanted their relationship to start.

"Mr. Wallace, I am sure you are eager to get started. But did you know a good breakfast gives you strength?"

On a more conciliatory note, she added, "Have you had your breakfast yet?"

He appeared nonplussed at her mild response, and muttered, "A cup of coffee was good enough for me."

Rose pointed to the opposite chair with a soft smile. "That will not do. You need a proper breakfast. Please sit, and I will serve you."

When his jaw hardened and his eyes cooled, she wagged her finger. "Now, now... don't do that. You need your strength, and I'm just doing what any good neighbor would do. I do not think you will get very far in the restaurant business if you don't take care of your health. Agreed?"

He toyed with the idea for a moment, then he

nodded. "Yes, you may be right. I should've thought of that."

Elated at her small victory, Rose hurried to serve him before the breakfast got cold. She hoped his hesitant smile would last the entire day.

CHAPTER 4

It didn't even last an hour. Rose decided Joseph had lost his senses. Either that or he had lost the art of what it meant to be reasonable or kind. He barked orders at the laborers and increased his demands by the minute.

Rose likened him to a monstrous officer on a naval ship with a crew of roughneck sailors at his command. He brooked no disagreements and refused any suggestions that clashed with his ideals. She didn't understand why Joseph acted in such a manner, but she wanted none of his bad behavior.

When they had left the house to drive to the restaurant, it had taken twenty minutes to navigate the populated part of town and find a good place to tie the buggy. The restaurant building stood in the heart of town near the largest bank, a well-stocked mercantile store and a luxury inn. The building itself resembled little more than a plain structure made of wood with wide front windows.

Inside the darkened interior, gathered around a makeshift table and two creaking chairs, Joseph laid out the plans. The drawings revealed the details of the tables and chairs, the hanging lamps, and the kitchen. Rose noted the proximity of the tables and chairs to the kitchen and thought there should be more space between them.

Before she voiced her idea on the matter, a tall, lanky laborer with a shock of red hair and a sweat-filled face approached. He cast a wary glance at Joseph's irritated face and said, "Uh... sir. Me and the boys were thinking you ought to put a little distance between them tables and the kitchen door. Might make it easier for when you want to serve them hot meals."

At Joseph's thunderous glare, Rose rushed to add, "What a good idea. I was thinking about the same thing. How wise of you to point it out."

The laborer gawked at Rose and bowed. "Uh... thank you, ma'am. Yes, thank you for listening."

When he scurried away with a gap-toothed grin, Joseph whirled on Rose. He lowered his voice to a furious whisper—mindful of the workers—and demanded, "Who gave you the right to do that?"

Rose did not hesitate in her response. "God did. I have the freedom to speak my mind, Joseph Wallace, and no man can take what the good Lord has given me. Not even you."

Her calm response checked his fury, and his eyes widened. When he struggled to come up with a suitable answer, Rose placed her hand over his own and spoke in low, calm tones. "Joseph, you are a fine man, and I know you've worked hard on this. Everyone here wants to help, and so do I, but you must let us speak our thoughts, even if we don't always agree."

He rolled the sheets of paper and tucked them into this jacket pocket with a grimace. "I guess you are right. Let's grab a bite to eat and come back later. I need a drink."

At her worried glance, he amended his comment: "Not like you're thinking. Just something to wet my throat."

Rose allowed him to lead her out of the restaurant. Just before she departed, she turned to the men and flashed a bright smile. When they smiled back, she gathered the strings of her bonnet and secured it. Joseph was right. There were lots of things to do and a short time to get them done. She only hoped one month was long enough. *Please God, help me bring a little joy into his life.*

CHAPTER 5

Two weeks later, Rose sensed that Joseph was turning over a new leaf. He still had bouts of anger, but he had tempered them to a large extent. Even the laborers commented on his change. Rose couldn't help feelings of pride on the part she'd played to help him. And she never stopped praying that Joseph could find the happiness he deserved.

That evening, he'd promised to come over to discuss the menu together. Rose felt content to share in this work with him, even if she longed to become a more permanent part of his life. The end of the month fast approached; she knew she'd have to leave him behind, but she wanted to savor the time left.

When he rushed into his parents' home with his tie askew, she clapped her hands. At his dumbfounded expression, she pointed to his neck. "This is the first time I have seen you, shall we say, less than suitably dressed."

He glanced at the offending material and brushed it aside with a quick grin. "No time for that now. I want you to see the menu. I've been going over it today with Mrs. Brown, the cook I have in mind, and she tells me she's not good at newfangled cooking. I think she hated it. Can you think of some way to improve this?"

Rose waved him over to the low-lying table in the drawing room and bent over the menu. She reviewed the items he'd listed in meticulous order and understood why Mrs. Brown had difficulties with his ideas…

Entrees

Artichokes a la Bretonne, Aubergine sur la grille, Absinthe creme, Aggysinas fanchonettes

Meats

Beef piece, au pain perdu, beef a la gelee, ou a la royale, beef roasted sirloin, aloyau a la broche, duck canetons de Rouen sauce a la orange

Biscuits

Biscuits a la Italienne, biscuits manqués a la fleur d'orange, biscuit de niauffes

Fish

Carp au blue ou au court bouillon, Carp fricandeau, Carp roes in jelly, aspic de laitances, Cod in dauphin

Dessert

Cheesecake, gateau au fromage, cherries en chemise, carrot cake a la Orleans, Charlotte de poms aux confitures—

Rose stopped reading. Some of the dishes were familiar, but many were strange—even to her. "Is this your menu? Do you plan to serve these meals?"

"Goodness no."

Rose's sigh of relief soon vanished at his boisterous reply.

"That is only the beginning. I have a longer list

than this one. Just thought I'd show you the basics first."

Rose examined the list again, thinking how to reply. Joseph might lose clientele before he even got started. She gentled her tone and smiled to soften the blow. "Joseph, I admire your wish to be different and stand out, but many of your clients will be lost with these dishes."

"What do you mean?"

His befuddled expression touched her heart, and Rose thought of the best way to explain. "Tell me this: what would you prefer to eat? A nice serving of Aunt Sally's sweet pudding, or a giant bite of cold calf's tongue ou a la royale?"

He made a face. "Aunt Sally's pudding is my bet."

Rose smiled. "I couldn't have said it better myself."

The point she tried to convey dawned on him, and he ran restless hands thought his hair. "Never thought of it like that."

Rose agreed with him. For all of his brilliance, he could be obtuse. "I know. But you are serving miners and their families. After a hard day's work, they would prefer to understand what they are eating instead of having someone tell them what it means."

He snapped is fingers at her logical comment and

his eyes brightened. "You're right. Will you help me put together a better menu? Let's do it tomorrow. I'll pick you up bright and early. Deal?"

His heartfelt request filled her with delight, and Rose melted. She'd go to the ends of the earth to see his smile. "Yes, it's a deal."

CHAPTER 6

THE NEXT MORNING, ROSE AWOKE EAGER TO GET started on Joseph's new menu. She rushed to eat her breakfast with one eye on the time and the other eye on the window.

When she heard the telltale wheels of the buggy roll up to the drive, she raced outside with a bright smile. When a laborer with a somber face appeared instead of Joseph's familiar form, she frowned. Where was he? Had there been an accident? Maybe he fell through the floor or a beam struck him on the head. Fear clogged her heart as she moved toward him.

"Is Joseph doing well? Did something happen to him?"

The laborer, called Ben, held his weathered hat in

his hands and lowered his shaggy head. "No, ma'am. He was coming to get ya, but a strange woman dropped by. He was for sure shocked to see 'er and he sent me to get ya instead."

A strange woman. Rose held her breath. Who might that be?

The drive to the restaurant seemed twice as long as the days before, but she struggled to stay calm. She held no claim on Joseph's affections, no matter how much she hoped for the contrary.

When they arrived, Rose rushed inside the door. The pungent scent of an expensive French perfume assailed her and stopped her in her tracks. The cloying smell filled the room and circled a vision draped in white.

Surprised at her poise and elegance, Rose watched the woman gush over Joseph with a sense of familiarity. The finest French gown clung to her willowy frame, and a white bonnet with white feathers adorned her shapely head. Tinkling laughter bubbled out of perfect lips and high cheeks shone in delight. Joseph appeared enraptured, if his stunned expression was any sign, and Rose staggered under the virulent sting of envy.

She was planning to slip away when Joseph spied her and motioned her over to his side. When he introduced the vision as Lacey Walker, Rose hovered like a fifth wheel on a rusted wagon. Miss Walker had no such inhibitions.

"Well, my stars, how do you do? It sure is nice to meet you. Joseph tells me you're from Maine and came all this way to marry him. How delightful."

Rose winced. The woman's way of saying *delightful* lacked a complimentary tone. "It is nice to meet you too, Miss Walker."

Lacey's smile widened, and she tapped Rose on the elbow with her frilly fan. "Oh, please, call me Lacey. Did Joseph tell you how well we knew—I should say *know*—each other?"

No, he didn't mention that pertinent piece of information. Rose did not understand why the woman spoke in such a spiteful way, but she answered on a polite note, "No, I am afraid he did not. He has been very busy with the restaurant."

She hoped her tone might end the conversation, but the woman's sharp glance caught the hurt buried in her eyes.

"Oh, darling. Don't worry over little old me. I'm just passing through on my way to Texas. Lots of holes out there need fancy places to eat."

Rose turned to Joseph at Lacey's subtle hint. His

eyes had frozen into wintergreen spikes, and deep furrows lined his cheeks.

As Lacey continued her reminiscence into the past, Rose rushed to jump in and hoped Joseph wouldn't flay her on the spot. "Miss Walker, I don't mean to interrupt, but we have a lot of work to do. The opening of the restaurant is just over a week away. Maybe Joseph can visit with you later?"

The younger woman hissed and her eyes narrowed. "You don't say." Her tone brimmed with contempt and she screeched, "Joseph, are you letting this helper of yours run me out of town?"

Joseph brushed off Lacey's fury and turned to Rose with a grateful glance. His eyes gleamed and he offered a sharp reply. "Yep, got lots to do. Run along, Lacey, and find another fool to waste his time."

Lacey stamped her foot and flounced away in a whirl of satin and silk. When she left, Rose heaved a deep sigh of relief, unaware that Joseph watched her.

"Don't worry Rose. She left me hanging at the altar a couple years ago, and I'd never want to tangle with that viper again."

Rose's mouth fell open, and she snapped it shut with a flush. "That's the woman that broke your heart?"

He winced. "Well, when you put it that way...yes,

it felt like it for a long time. But seeing her again made me realize it was just a fancy. Nothing real or with substance. Now, is my menu up to snuff or what?"

Rose's smile widened at his brusque change of subject. *Oh, Joseph, I'm so glad I haven't lost you.*

CHAPTER 7

THE REST OF THE DAYS PASSED BY IN A BLUR, AND soon, opening night arrived. Rose calmed her jitters and took special care with her appearance.

She wore a soft pink and cream evening dress that hugged the gentle curve of her waist and fell in silken folds. The V-shaped neckline with encrusted pearls and ruffled capped sleeves had been a gift from her sister. It was the finest garment she owned. At the last minute, she let her hair flow free and didn't notice how much it enhanced her ethereal glow.

When she arrived, Rose found a bright blue ribbon barred the way. A crowd had gathered, and soon the silken banner lay in two pieces after Joseph did the honors. A brief speech followed rounds of toasting and greetings, and the crowd gravitated inside.

The restaurant glowed with freshly painted shutters in forest green trimmed in red. A sign with the name *The Golden River* hung in shimmering letters over a bright stained glass door.

Rose stepped over the threshold and held her breath. A polished mahogany floor with tasteful oriental rugs lay under three-tiered chandeliers. Etched glass covered the side walls, and curved oak tables with matching chairs stood in neat circles. The upholstered chairs matched the shutters for a more uniform look, and long curtains hung over tall windows with gold braiding.

Rose noted the floral arrangements with candles in the centers of the tables and gasped in delight. It had been her idea to place scented flowers with a perfumed candle as an added touch, but she thought Joseph hadn't cared for the idea. How wrong she had been.

Her eyes sought his elegant form. She found him among the Wallace clan, and marveled at their well-dressed appearance. Her reserved seat waited, and she sat in anticipation. The first dish came and Rose cheered just like everyone else. She felt proud of how well things had turned out.

Joseph ambled over to her table an hour later and collapsed beside her with a wide grin. "Enjoyed your meal?"

Rose placed an impulsive kiss on his cheek. She ignored the flash of surprise in his eyes and said, "How wonderful everything is tonight. I loved every bite, and the cheesecake was exquisite. Tell Mrs. Brooks she can cook for me any day."

He nodded and glanced at the kitchen door. "I will do that. Before I forget, I just wanted to thank you for your help. I couldn't have done it without you, and that's the truth."

Rose's heart wallowed in bliss. She longed to share her love with Joseph, but she didn't want to speak out of turn. He still hadn't told her his feelings, but she hoped he had changed his mind about their marriage.

"Rose, I have something for you."

When his eyes darkened and he lowered his voice, Rose leaned forward. She watched him reach into this jacket and her spirit soared on the wings of hope. At last, he would propose and ask her to be his bride. Excitement pounded through her veins, and she placed her hands against her chest to calm the thundering beats. Thoughts of a happy life together and the children to come filled her with delight. She wanted to be a part of his family and tell him how much he meant to—

"This is the reference I promised you. I added extra details to make sure you find work at any school, or can even open your own school."

Rose froze. The sound of wedding bells broke and shattered. A gong peeled in her ear and the clanging sound increased. She shivered and pulled her scarf closer. At her dumfounded expression, Joseph rushed to explain: "I can go myself and give a personal reference if needed. All you need to do is say the word, and I'll be there."

No, you won't. A dense cloud of unhappiness overwhelmed her, and Rose stumbled to her feet. The expected outcome of the evening was her fault, and she accepted the blame. She had no right for such high expectations, but her foolish heart had imagined things differently. Words of gratitude clung to her lips, but she didn't have the strength to utter them.

She ignored Joseph's cry of concern as she ran from the room in a swirl of hurt. *Dear God, please help me bear this pain.*

CHAPTER 8

ONE WEEK LATER

Joseph watched the bright orb of the moon from the porch swing. Sleep hadn't come in days, and left him gritty eyed and out of sorts. The cool air provided a fresh perspective to his tortured thoughts, but didn't ease the pain in his heart. *Why can't I get her disappointed face out of my mind?*

He had bungled the entire affair, and his lips twisted into a bitter smile. What a fool he had been to see the truth too late. His life did not bear living without Rose's guiding presence and bright smile. When he went to his parents' home to tell her, she refused to see him or talk to him. His father had taken her side and glared at Joseph, and even his mother had been less than pleased.

Joseph leaned forward and curled his hands under his chin. His father had relented after a few days and told him Rose was leaving on the morning train. The idea sickened him and spurred him to action. She couldn't leave him—not now. *Wait for me, Rose. I'm coming to get you.*

CHAPTER 9

ROSE DRAGGED HERSELF TO THE CONDUCTOR'S window and bought a ticket to Maine. He noticed her red-rimmed eyes and wet cheeks, but refrained from commenting. She had seen other furtive glances cast her way, but didn't have the heart to pretend. Home was a haven for a broken heart, and she couldn't wait to leave.

She sat on the platform bench, her eyes bonded to the planks of wood. Maybe she could get a teaching job after she got back. Lots of children needed her help, and she needed theirs. It would be wonderful to feel—

Two pairs of gleaming boots stepped into her line of view. Her eyes rose to a well-fitted suit, a perfect tie, until it locked on the mournful eyes of

Joseph Wallace. Rose gasped at his grey-tinged face; he seemed to have aged ten years. Heavy eyes, deep-grooved cheeks, and a haggard appearance damp-ened his good looks. Her heart moved and she couldn't stop her yelp of surprise. "Joseph, are you ill? What is wrong? Do you need a doctor? Please tell me."

"No Rose. I need *you*."

Rose blinked, wondering if she had heard wrong. She stood in his shadow, her eyes devouring his face. When he repeated himself, she expelled a deep breath. "What did you say?"

"I need you. Then I will be whole again."

The chains shattered from around her heart and Rose reeled from the impact. The days of hurt and uncertainty melted away. Happiness swamped her in an overflow and she flew into his arms with a joyful cry.

"Are you sure, Joseph? Please don't offer your heart if you aren't sure. I cannot take"—her voice cracked and wobbled— "another disappointment."

His chest rumbled against her cheek. "Yes, I am sure. And no, you will never have to doubt again. I am a Wallace and we don't do things in half measures. My word stands on my honor as a gentleman."

He placed a hand under his chin and his eyes locked on hers. "Never leave me again, do you hear? And I promise I will love you forever."

Rose closed her eyes and allowed the moment to overtake her. She had countless things she wanted to say, but they were drawing a crowd. Onlookers clapped, some shielded their eyes, others laughed, and the children made faces.

"I guess we had better go somewhere else so I can tell you how I feel."

Joseph released her with a grin and swung her carryall over his shoulder. "I have a great idea. Let's grab a bite to eat at the restaurant, and then we will visit my parents to tell them the good news."

He held out his right hand to shake her own, and Rose glanced at him curiously.

"Deal?"

Rose smothered her laughter, remembering how they'd first met. She placed her hand in his own with delight and whispered, "Yes, my darling. It's a deal."

THE END

Faith-Ann Smith has always loved to write. As a child, she enjoyed penning simple tales about prairie life in her home state of Oklahoma. While in college, Faith-Ann became fascinated with American history, particularly of the 19th century, and began to write creative historical fiction in her late twenties. Blessed with a loving husband and two precious children, Faith-Ann enjoys knitting, teaching Sunday School and tending to the flower beds surrounding her home in Nebraska.

To keep up to date with her latest releases, you may visit www.hopemeadowpublishing.com and sign up for her newsletter.

FREE STORY!

For a FREE sweet historical romance e-book, please
sign up for Hope Meadow Publishing's newsletter at
www.hopemeadowpublishing.com

CPSIA information can be obtained
at www.ICGtesting.com
Printed in the USA
BVHW072215010520
579061BV00002B/690

9 781098 632434